PURIFIED

PURIFIED

BRIAN ROBERT SMITH

3²³**ooks**

Toronto, Canada

Canadian Intellectual Property Office Registration Number: 1109080
Library of Congress Registration Number: TXu 1-869-923
ISBN (paperback first edition): 978-0-9920483-3-4

Published by 323 Books

Printed in the U. S. A.

Cover Design by Derek Murphy

DEDICATION

For the two that have supported and encouraged this
incredible, creative adventure.

My wife, Sonia.
My mother-in-law, Claudette.

PART I

THE ESCAPE

CHAPTER 1

It was extreme pride and a little boredom that motivated a grocer to tidy his sidewalk fruit stand. He turned his head to see light traffic moving slowly through the downtown section of this tired, tranquil town. Small stores lined both sides of the street along with people in no great hurry to go about their daily business. This place hadn't moved a day past 1960, and the grocer was just fine with that.

He left the fruit stand and watched a young mother who pushed her two kids in a modern double stroller. She stopped to window shop the display of a woman's fashion store. A couple strolled along the sidewalk, blocking the grocer's view. He watched them as they moved along. He noticed that they were more interested in their new romance than the shops they passed.

He took a broom leaning beside the door to unnecessarily

sweep the path for an older couple. A smile and a friendly back pat from the old gentleman made it obvious they had known each other for a long time.

The lights changed at an intersection nearby causing cars to stop in front of him, all except a blue van that surged to make it through. The grocer shook his head in disgust before turning away. He followed the couple into his store.

***

Andrew manhandled the steering wheel to maneuver the van in and out of traffic, finding challenge in what little congestion there was. He surged away from all his apparent obstructions—the winner of nothing.

He peered into the rear view mirror while he enjoyed his recklessness. Unorganized medical equipment shook including a stretcher that looked like it would become airborne any second. He was most interested in Steve who sat on a bag of sand. Andrew watched Steve shake his head while trying to keep things in one place. Steve muttered to himself, "An empty, shaking bed. Where's the future in that?"

Andrew cranked the wheel to round a corner. Stuff behind him crashed which brought a smirk to his overzealous, race car driver face.

"Shit, man. You're gonna bust my head back here," Steve said.

"I'll get the next one right. Promise," Andrew replied with a sarcastic smile. He proceeded to take another sharp corner then drove over a high curb. He quickly looked back into the rear view so he wouldn't miss Steve being tossed again.

"Come on, Andrew."

Andrew motored along, unconcerned about Steve's discomfort. He floored the gas on a straightaway resembling a drag strip for one with his destination up ahead. It was a driveway but Andrew didn't slow down to make the turn. The target defined itself quickly exposing a parking lot and a building. He tapped the brakes lightly and pulled the steering wheel hard to ensure a fishtail entry. Success, despite the unseen, moaning passenger bouncing around in the back.

The van screeched to a grinding halt. Andrew was shocked. His hands froze to the wheel like he was shot with a stun gun for careless driving.

"Holy shit," Steve said from behind Andrew.

Out the front window was a sign announcing Rocksbrough Funeral Home. The parking lot was full. Police cruisers were everywhere.

Andrew remained still, unsure what his next move should be. He scanned the parking lot. Neither he nor Steve moved or said anything. From the side view mirror, Andrew noticed a cruiser behind the van. "Shit, man, a cop. Now what?" he said as though he needed an answer but didn't really expect one.

"Just one?" Steve said sarcastically.

"Behind us." Andrew spun around, suddenly breaking from his paralyzed position. "They've got nothin' on us," he claimed despite not being accused of anything. He slammed the transmission in park and rushed to the back window for a closer look. "What are they gonna nail us for? There's nothin' in here but ticker tape and a rolling bed."

He watched the cruiser continue around the van. Andrew stumbled back to the driver's seat. The cruiser stopped at the front door. An officer got out. He took a second to look around the area and at the van, but he never locked eyes with Andrew.

Andrew kept the van stopped while the cop pocketed his sunglasses. He entered the funeral home.

"Just two guys in a van. Nothin' wrong with that. Yet," Andrew said with sudden sarcasm.

CHAPTER 2

Inside, the officer immediately encountered plain clothed and uniformed officers who filled the lobby of this tastefully decorated funeral home. They talked in groups with light conversations and soft laughter. Really, these guys were doing all they could to hold back from their usual tough guy camaraderie. The officer said nothing and slipped into a group without any type of greeting or introduction.

He saw couples quietly socializing near the entrance of another room. Unlike himself, who felt it necessary to be there for ass kissing duty, these people looked like they were here to pay their legitimate respects but were forced to wait due to an overwhelming turnout.

He ignored the conversation of the group he was in and watched a woman wipe a tear from her cheek as she left the other room. Her husband followed close behind to comfort her as they made their way slowly through the crowd. He watched them come toward him, but they were forced to stop. The group he was with had gotten loud, and they blocked the entrance door. At first no one noticed the couple, but the officer cleared a path. Others quieted, realizing instantly their inappropriate behavior considering the circumstances.

***

Andrew stopped the van abruptly after backing into the funeral home garage bay, beside a hearse. He was out of the van before the engine completed its sputtering stop. Between the van and the hearse, he made his way to the back of the garage. Unlike upstairs, there was nothing elegant here. Some spare tires were stacked in the corner. Car parts hung from the ceiling joists. He approached a work bench that stretched across the back wall. It was littered with traffic pylons and funeral procession signs among other stuff. All of that went well with the damaged caskets stacked on top of each other along an adjacent wall.

***

The double doors of the van flew open with a crash of equipment. Steve rushed out. He took a straight path to a closed door separating the garage from another unseen room. With slight hesitation, he grabbed the handle and pulled the door open.

He burst into a spotless preparation room. This room's tidiness, and respect for what was going on in here, made him stop his aggressive entrance as soon as he entered.

He met eye to eye with Dr. Henry Harlow who tried to move a body on an embalming table while he entertained himself by whistling a merry tune. He struggled with the weight and seemed relieved that he now had help. He slid quickly along the white tiled floor to the other side of the table—a silent invitation for Steve's assistance. Dr. Harlow smiled keenly and impatiently. Steve easily overlooked his geeky awkwardness because he knew he was dealing with a genius, but Dr. Harlow's buggy eyes told a very different story. Steve sighed with the thought that Dr. Harlow was insane.

Steve didn't move from the entrance. He started to talk but quickly stopped himself. Instead, he shook his head. Reluctantly he claimed, "It's a damn crime scene up there. We can't…"

Dr. Harlow quickly turned to the marble counter top. He slammed into one of the opened white cabinet doors that blocked him from getting to Steve. He banged into the table during his erratic attempt to get around it. That caused the third arm of the corpse to helplessly fall over the side, but Dr. Harlow didn't seem to care or even notice. He grabbed Steve by the shoulders. "Do you feel the thrill, the rush, the power? Nothin' on the street gets ya this wired."

Steve stared straight into Dr. Harlow's eyes. He couldn't

help but notice the void beyond. Somewhere from within that empty space, Dr. Harlow continued, "Better than the drugs in Nam."

***

In a room decorated with fine furniture, classic art work, and overwhelmed with funeral bouquets, Detective Warren Fillmore stood in front of a casket. His wife, Linda, lay inside. He watched her quietly with a youthful authority he possessed despite his current state of overwhelming grief. He repositioned Linda's hands, taking a second to touch her wedding ring. He touched her face; stroked her blond hair. His face showed no trace of the hurt he felt inside, although a tear trickled down his cheek which he made no attempt to wipe clear.

A friend touched Warren lightly on the shoulder. His presence did nothing to break Warren away from the trance he currently had on his deceased wife. He didn't notice the man leave, but he did know his mother was now beside him. She hugged him softly as they both looked at the lifelessness in front of them.

"She's moved on, dear," his mother whispered. This broke Warren from the past even though he wasn't ready to let go.

He looked up and the room was suddenly silent. People turned from their conversations. Others got up from the couches and high back chairs. Everyone watched him. He felt everyone sharing his grief. He knew everyone felt his loss. He was guided slowly by his mother into the room where well-wishers engulfed him.

***

Dr. Harlow wedged the preparation room door open as Steve presented a wall of objections.

"It's bloody suicide to go through with it," Steve said.

Dr. Harlow ignored him. He rushed to the van where Andrew straightened up the contents disturbed by Steve's harsh departure.

"Come on, Doctor, think for a second," Andrew said.

Dr. Harlow ignored him also and began to move a sandbag from the van, but his frail body was incapable.

Dr. Harlow turned from the sandbag with messed hair and wiped drool from his mouth. He snarled at Andrew, "There, I gave you two." He tried to move the bag again. "Help here, please."

***

The Funeral Director, Mr. Amos, stood at the door of the main room. "Excuse me, ladies and gentlemen."

People stopped their conversations and gave their attention to Mr. Amos.

"At this time, Linda's family would like to spend time alone with her." Mr. Amos stepped into the room. "A funeral service and burial will be held tomorrow morning at eleven in

11

Linda's home town of Lordstown."

Immediately, people obeyed and made their way to the door where Mr. Amos politely thanked them for their cooperation. He watched Warren, and a small group of his family, remain close to the casket.

***

Andrew stood motionless second guessing whether he should unload the stretcher. "Well, either way, to me it makes no difference. It's not like this is our first time." He continued to unsecure the stretcher from the van floor.

He watched Steve reluctantly drop a bag of sand on some others.

"But it's the first time we have the Police Man's Ball for an audience," Steve said.

Andrew looked back to see Dr. Harlow in the preparation room. He was happily whistling then interrupted himself with incoherent mumbling while he packed up some equipment.

Andrew noticed Steve watching him too.

"And shit, Andrew. We're doing it with a madman who can't even tell the difference between a tooth brush and a hair comb." Steve turned away and aggressively grabbed on to another bag.

"Well, I guess that's what happens when a genius is ignored," Andrew said with raised eyebrows.

Steve snorted. "Ignored? Is that what you call it? I will give you the genius part though." He continued to move the sand bag with a shake of his head.

Andrew hesitated with the bed. He took another look at Dr. Harlow. He shrugged and aggressively pulled the bed from its supports.

***

While still acting as a doorman, Mr. Amos watched Warren walk slowly to the door, surrounded by his family. Nobody walked alone, and nobody looked back. Just as Mr. Amos scripted, their time with Linda was over. Only the process of her burial remained. For now though, his patience with this group of people dealing with their current loss was most important.

As Warren left the room, Mr. Amos made his way toward the casket. He began to close the lid. He adjusted some flowers that blocked the latch. Just before the lid shut, Linda's arm twitched. Mr. Amos stopped. He looked back to see if anyone was still there. Satisfied he was alone, he opened the lid a crack higher. Everything seemed fine. He sighed, realizing he was just imagining things. He noticed a rose petal in Linda's hair. He opened the lid higher then reached in.

She blinked.

***

An elevator door in the preparation room opened. Mr. Amos frantically dashed out leaving the closed casket inside.

He panicked while looking for someone to help. He saw Dr. Harlow and rushed to him. "She's alive."

Mesmerized, Dr. Harlow calmly stated, "I know. She's perfect."

Mr. Amos turned as Andrew and Steve stepped into the preparation room. They looked at each other when they saw the casket and Mr. Amos. Andrew stepped toward him.

"Shouldn't she still be saying goodbye?" He turned back to Steve with a smirk. "There's no room for the dead down here yet. We're not—"

Mr. Amos pushed past Andrew and rushed to Steve. He forced him toward the casket. "She's awake. My God, Steve, she's…"

Mr. Amos breathed a sigh of relief when Andrew and Steve snapped into action. He watched them quickly roll the casket into the room. Without hesitation, Andrew opened it.

Mr. Amos's panic suddenly returned when Linda gasped for air. She grabbed Andrew like she was the jaws of death. Instantly, he was totally smothered as she ripped and clawed her way out. Andrew tried his best to control her, but she had the advantage of desperation on her side.

Steve jumped in to even the odds then Dr. Harlow injected her.

The attack stopped. Mr. Amos watched nervously expecting another surge. There was nothing.

Mr. Amos stepped back as Steve ran past him and into the garage. Mr. Amos spun back around. Andrew was getting Linda out from the casket. As if rehearsed to perfection,

Steve rolled the stretcher beside the casket and helped Andrew get Linda on it. Mr. Amos moved out of the way as he helplessly watched them push the stretcher into the garage and straight into the van. Dr. Harlow followed and jumped in pulling the double doors shut. Andrew went to the driver's door; Steve, the passenger side.

Mr. Amos made reluctant eye contact with Steve. Steve sighed then jumped in the van and slammed the door shut. The van started. It jolted forward, then it was gone.

Mr. Amos stood short of breath in the doorway. He backed up against the door to help his balance. He looked at the empty casket; at the mutated corpse in the other room.

CHAPTER 3

Mason Bushing breathed heavily as he stood flat against the wall of a building. He was sure he had been seen escaping, but he didn't know by who or from where they would be coming after him. He was convinced about one thing though, soon he wouldn't be alone.

He had never been outside this building. His sudden exposure to the dark, dreary landscape left him confused and disoriented, but he didn't care. For Mason, there was no turning back. He was done with being held down here.

The door he just came from was closed, but he was certain it would burst open any moment. This short lived isolation was a feeling he wished he could hold on to for eternity. Considering what he had been through during the past year, the freedom he was now experiencing, and getting back what he had lost, was his holy grail.

Mason looked into the darkness. Only lights from another larger building helped him see his surroundings. A field, a country road—otherwise black.

Dr. Harlow staggered out from the door, obviously exhausted. This wasn't the threat Mason expected, but a threat nonetheless. Mason snarled, partly in preparation for the imminent battle, but mostly because of the interrupted solitude he enjoyed so briefly. The snarl gave up Mason's position so he lunged. They both fell to the ground in a tangle of arms and legs.

Mason ended up on top, easily outmaneuvering and overpowering Dr. Harlow. Although Mason could end this matchup right away, he hesitated. The man under him was old, frail, and slippery—like a snake in a white lab coat.

Dr. Harlow managed to break free. Mason watched him turn away and fumble through his coat pockets. This gave him another chance, but he didn't act fast enough. Dr. Harlow spun back around and held up a scalpel, slashing it with the accuracy of a crazed lunatic. "Sorry, Mason, but I can't let you leave." He stepped closer.

Mason replied with defiance. "Save me or kill me. You can't make up your mind?"

Dr. Harlow looked at the scalpel. He dropped it. "I have great plans for you." He took another step toward Mason. He showed his hands then reached out.

"Your plans, your experiment… Your insanity."

Dr. Harlow's nose flared. His eyes opened wide. "It's not an experiment, Mason. It's reality. You're proof of that."

Mason went for the scalpel, but Dr. Harlow stepped on it. Mason knocked him to the ground.

Dr. Harlow went down hard, but close to the scalpel. He grabbed it. As Mason surged, he saw Dr. Harlow reluctantly hold it up. It would certainly penetrate, but he threw it toward a sewer grate a short distance away. It fell between the cracks.

Dr. Harlow pleaded, "Why, Mason, after all I've done for you?" He held up his arms to protect himself from the sure impact.

Mason's body smothered him. This time he wasn't going to hold back. "You, saving my life, took my life away," Mason said with fire in his eyes. "Being your prisoner isn't how I plan to get it back."

Mason saw Andrew appear from the corner of the building just as he was ready to take Dr. Harlow out of this equation. He looked to the field, then back. Andrew was running toward him. Mason pushed himself away from Dr. Harlow. He turned back to the field and quickly considered his options.

He began to run.

The surgical gown he wore flapped around his legs with every stride. He felt the impact from rocks beneath his bare feet, but that didn't stop Mason.

"There's no use trying to escape, Mason. You're miles from anywhere," Dr. Harlow shouted desperately.

Mason continued into the field.

"Time to return to the grave, dead man," Andrew added.

"You have no clothes, no food, no money. You need me," Dr. Harlow yelled. "You're dead, Mason."

Mason ignored them and continued running aimlessly over what he couldn't see.

Suddenly, Mason grabbed his head and fell to his knees. His head rang—screeched inside, to the point of feeling like it would explode. Despite the nauseating sensation, he struggled to get back up.

He started moving again, but he was disoriented. At first the feeling strengthened, so he surged another way. Nothing changed. He looked up, and his head spun. He staggered. He tried to steady himself and focus on what he could see. Something was in front of him, but it was just a blur. He knew for sure nothing should be where he was going, so he turned sharply and bolted in the opposite direction.

Almost immediately, the screeching in his head weakened. He focused on running in a straight line, and with that, the sensation stopped. That motivated him to move faster.

Ahead was the field and the darkness he pursued in the first place. His vision was clear now. The ringing was gone. He knew what was behind him, and he never looked back.

CHAPTER 4

Mason sat on a rock along the edge of a small creek with his feet soaking in the water. He wasn't really trying to get them clean, or soothe the soreness, or anything like that. They just happened to be in the water. There was nothing on them, so they were soaking.

He watched his reflection—a young man that kept getting torn apart with every surge of energy the water offered. The face he looked at was much different than the one he remembered the last time he had the luxury of reflection. He was much thinner than before. He wondered if this was permanent, or if he could get back what he once had. This was the first time he had considered any of this. He had just spent considerable time as a prisoner of Dr. Harlow that had nothing to do with the past or the future. It had been all about what was happening to him then, and how he was going to get out of there.

Maybe Dr. Harlow had been right. *Why, Mason, after all I've done for you?* He remembered himself a year ago dying in a hospital bed. There was no freedom there either. There was no past or future. Just dealing again with what was happening, and how he would get through it—if he would get through it. Then, when the lights went out, Dr. Harlow gave him the answer. He called it Purify, and as far as Mason could tell, it worked. At least it did for him. Others had been with him, but he didn't know when they came. He had no idea how they got there, or if they had been dead before. Hell, he didn't know how he got there, but he was pretty sure he had died.

It was that feeling of the end that conflicted with Mason after he realized his life was not over. What happened, and what was happening, just didn't feel right. He had been dying when he wanted to live. He was alive when he should be dead. In what he'd once thought were his final moments, his death had been a sure thing. He hadn't had any strong feelings about what would come next, if anything at all. But here he was, and he knew for sure what was happening simply was not in the cards.

He felt as though he had just cheated death, but it hadn't been because of anything he did. Before any of this happened, the last thing Mason could remember had been that infamous white sheet about to be pulled over his head. But in the blink of an eye, he was conscious in what seemed like a very low budget medical lab. This told him someone else had taken control. When? He had no idea. How? He had no idea. Why? That, Mason knew. If what was done, could be done, then why not? Which left, who did all of this? That, no doubt, was Dr. Harlow.

At first Mason didn't know what to think of Dr. Harlow. He seemed genuine enough. Kind, caring, definitely devoted to what he had been doing; but it wasn't long before Mason realized everything was wrong. It all became crystal clear the work being done was unauthorized, underground. Mason didn't know what type of expertise Dr. Harlow had. He didn't know why this had all been happening. He didn't know what exactly Dr. Harlow had done to him, or if he had been doing the same thing to everyone else. There was one thing Mason did know for sure though. No one was leaving. The purified were there for good.

That's what didn't make sense to Mason. How could a—*a genius*—capable of doing what Dr. Harlow was doing, not see he wasn't giving new life, he was injecting them with death itself? He was holding them against their will. To Mason, that made the gift he had just been given, not worth getting at all. At first he thought he would stay there for a while to be sure everything was okay. Dr. Harlow would monitor his progress then send him back into the wild when he knew his patient was ready for the real world again. But as time went on, he realized there had been no plan for any type of release. This was prison to Mason. His crime had been death itself, and he had been sentenced with life.

Mason's relationship with Dr. Harlow turned when he

started speaking out about this exact point. At first those arguments were pointed directly at Dr. Harlow, but he could only see the fact that everyone there should be dead. He figured they had him to thank, or praise, for that. He couldn't see that holding them prisoner had taken away their basic right of freedom, and Mason couldn't bear living like that. Mason knew the value of what he had received, but he in no way felt indebted. He hadn't asked for this. He hadn't even bought into it during his last breath. He had been recruited, taken—stolen from his final resting place and brought there to be worked on like some kind of human test case.

Mason strongly believed that Dr. Harlow didn't give a shit about him or anyone else there. He only cared about his experiment. An experiment that obviously had no respect, or acceptance, in the medical community. Maybe the whole medical world had no knowledge of this at all, and Dr. Harlow was keeping it to himself. Maybe they knew Dr. Harlow as the nut case he was, so he had to take it underground to carry out his dream. If any of this had been the case, there was no chance of being rescued or anything like that. The more Mason thought about it, the more he realized that if he was going to get out, it would have to be by escaping.

Mason tried to get others to see his point, arrange a mutiny of sorts, but they were reluctant. Instead of rising up against the all mighty doctor, they had thoughts of their own. They were alive at least, prisoners, but alive. This reluctance made it difficult for Mason to get everyone on board. It also made it difficult to keep his plans quiet, but he tried in secret meetings and hushed conversations. Some discussions got heated and had to be left unsolved. Some had taken off in completely different directions than Mason had intended. He tried desperately to keep things focused on a simple escape plan, but too many opinions made that next to impossible.

Originally, Mason wanted everyone to bolt from the place, all at the same time. There were five of them, four men and one woman. He remembered the woman well—Hazel. She, by no means, would hold them back. With Andrew and Steve being their only significant challenge, Mason had been prepared to take on one of them, and Hazel could probably handle the other. That left three men to deal with the frail, old doctor. How much easier could it be, Mason kept stressing. But the more he talked about it, the more they second guessed the idea.

They were mainly concerned about two things. What would they do if something physically went wrong, and who exactly were they? At least under the care of Dr. Harlow, there had been hope of getting through this whole thing in one piece. On their own, any problem would surely be the end again. The other pressing concern had taken up most of those heated conversations and had been responsible for the many diversions. It had been the big *who* question. The person they were before was dead, so who were they now? A least, who would everyone else think they were? If they broke away, how would any of them handle this?

Mason didn't want to hear any of that. He had been in the

moment—no past and no future. He would have plenty of time to think once he made a clean break. But he hadn't been winning the argument, so he was forced to make another plan.

That plan included Bob Robinson who had been on board all along. At least it seemed like he was, but someone tipped Dr. Harlow, or those damn flunkies of his, off. The thought of that took Mason away from staring at the broken image of himself in the water. He grabbed on to the only thing he had—the surgical gown.

"Fuck. God damn it you bastards."

This wasn't supposed to go down like this. He was supposed to have food, clothes, water. He slammed both fists into the creek leaving himself drenched and on both knees. He wasn't supposed to be alone. He wasn't supposed to be hiding in the woods. He was supposed to be the hero who saved everyone, but no one was free. They still remained captured under Dr. Harlow's oppressive care, and this was hardly what Mason himself considered liberty. He was supposed to pick up his life right where he left it. It wasn't much, but it was the only thing he had ever wanted. He wasn't supposed to be still dead to the rest of the world and dying all over again.

He looked up with water streaming down his face like a waterfall of tears. He stared at the decaying remains of a half-eaten rabbit lying within rocks on the other side of the creek. He took some deep, heavy breaths. He cleared the water from his face and placed the surgical gown to restore what little dignity he had left. He stepped out of the water and looked to the road in the distance. With the sun setting, a corn field and a farm house appeared vulnerable on the other side.

CHAPTER 5

After being camouflaged by tall corn stalks, Mason stepped out of the field and stood at its edge. He looked at the house and a barn next to it. He knelt down to keep himself concealed while he considered his options, or if he was really going to do what he was thinking of doing at all.

Breaking out of Dr. Harlow's immortality prison was one thing, but this was breaking in—a home invasion really. Sure, he had heard about desperate situations pushing people to do things they never thought they were capable of. But this? He knew he was tough enough for the job, but something of this nature had never fallen within his moral standards before.

He looked hard at the house and then at the gown he was now the proud owner of. *Do I go in ferociously, in my white nightgown; or take a more subtle approach, and scare the shit out of them as the ghost in white cotton?* He shook that thought out of his head with a slight smile then turned his attention to the barn.

Probably, this was a better option. How hard could it be to invade a barn? Or how wrong was it? Anything he could find in there was probably not being used anyway.

Mason began to walk across the open space between the corn field and the barn. The thought of getting caught tiptoeing through the dirt in a gown worried him almost as much as entering a building he had no right to be in. It wasn't much distance to cover, but it was wide open. He was the brightest thing within five miles in any direction.

He stopped at a small door beside the large garage door that provided machinery access into the barn. He looked back to the house before he did anything; back to the corn field; back to the road he could barely see because it was so far away. He tried the door. It was unlocked. With slight hesitation, he pushed it open. It creaked loudly, so he grabbed for the handle. He held it and froze to be sure quiet surrounded him. Satisfied that he wasn't caught before any crime was committed, he gently slipped around the door.

It was quiet inside and pitch dark. Mason left the door slightly open and cautiously walked in. After his eyes slowly adjusted, he made out a large space with a tractor parked and tools toward the back. *Awesome, no horses*. He walked along a wall trying to see what lay against it. Suddenly, something moved in front of him. *Shit*. He stopped walking instantly as an animal brushed between his legs. He jumped back. A cat screeched and hissed then ran out the door. Mason breathed heavily and sighed while he watched the door. He turned back to the wall and saw a pair of overalls.

***

Through the small opening left from the barn door, Mason stepped out with the overalls on. He took a second to check them out since there was at least some light here. *Not bad, considering*. His feet were bare though. Although the overalls were a nice start, it was really shoes he needed. The barn came up empty for that.

He looked along the ground and saw the cat watching the door while it tried to hide against a wall. The cat looked up and stared Mason down like it was going to rush him any second, but Mason could tell it was losing interest. All it really wanted was to get back inside the barn. It made a move for the door, but Mason's counter movement sent it scurrying in the opposite direction. *That's right, be afraid. No more pajama man here*. He watched it dash through the dirt until it was out of sight. Mason looked up to the house straight ahead. He thought if the cat could make it over there undetected, he should be able to also.

This crossing wasn't nearly as open as the trip to the barn, but still, stepping out there to get to the house was more risk than he wanted to take. However, his feet... Probably right behind the front door he was looking at, were shoes, or boots, or slippers; whatever. There should at least be something better than the nothing he was currently walking on. So he made the decision to go for another crossing, but more importantly, to find out what was behind that door.

Each step closer made him wonder if he was doing the right thing. Did he have any other option? Did he really need shoes? At the wooden step, which put him within arm's reach away from the handle, he wondered if he could open the door at all. The temptation overwhelmed him. His heart pounded, fueled with adrenaline. He took another step.

Mason stood with his hand on the handle. He turned it. The door opened. He looked through a small opening. Right in front of him was a pair of shoes and boots. He opened the door wider, exposing not much of the house—only this small entrance and a closet.

Without enough time to consider the benefits of shoes versus boots, a dog started barking. Mason couldn't see it, but he heard it coming. Its speed was obvious. Its weight pounded the floor boards. He knew for sure this was not something that sat on anyone's lap.

"Bo!" a man shouted. "You hear something, Bo?" There was more shuffling, along with the charging dog.

Mason looked down at the shoes.

"Go get it, boy."

Mason suddenly saw Bo, in the room just beyond the entrance and coming straight for him. Bo was a fierce, black guard dog with, what was obvious to Mason, focused intentions to attack. The man was not far behind. Mason made eye contact with him.

"Oh, look at that. A stranger calling in the night." The

man revealed a shot gun, engaged the dreaded pump, and pointed it at Mason; all in one motion. "Well, around here, we know just how to make you feel unwelcome."

Mason looked back to the shoes. He made a move to back away then hesitated. Swiftly, he bent down, grabbed the shoes, and closed the door. Bo slammed up against it. Mason turned—the field; or the long, open driveway? He held a shoe in each hand and ran for the field.

The last time he'd covered this distance, it had seemed like he was crossing a two lane highway. Now it felt like he was running end zone to end zone on two football fields. He reached the corn and looked back to see Bo running toward him—a mass of black and teeth. He also saw the man standing on the porch with the shotgun aimed.

Mason ran through the corn, turned into a row, and moved quickly along it. It was dark and congested. He could barely see anything in front of him. He could hear the mad rustling of corn behind him. Mason tried to look back to see how much distance he had on Bo, but he got pelted with corn stocks when he veered off track. He quickly got back in the row and accelerated. Unfortunately, he could still hear Bo, and he seemed faster.

Mason ran deeper into the field crossing row after row trying to shake Bo. The corn slapped his face like the flipping pages from a book, but it didn't slow him down. There was only one end to this race if he didn't get this dog off his ass. He fled down another row and tried to sneak a peek again. He succeeded this time. No assaulting corn stocks, and no

Bo.

Nothing could hold Mason back as he burst out from the field holding a shoe in each hand. Suddenly, he lost his footing and fell into a ditch. He tumbled, rolled, and ended up face down in runoff water. With aggressive barking being his main motivator, he scrambled back onto his feet as Bo exited the field. Mason bolted forward and instantly realized he only held one shoe. Frantically, he searched through the grass; through fist deep water, but he found nothing. He looked back and saw the shoe on the downgrade that caused him to trip. Unfortunately, Bo was too close. He dropped the other shoe and ran for the road.

Screeching tires and blinding headlights stopped Mason dead in his tracks. He stared at a truck inches from him. The man, hugging his shotgun, stared back. Bo covered some distance, growling in full pursuit. Mason staggered then gained his balance. He moved quickly toward the creek.

Immediately, Mason ran into ankle deep water then across to the other side. He plowed through dense bush without any consideration for what he might run into. He heard Bo splashing then branches breaking.

Mason stopped suddenly and turned. It was too dark to see Bo completely, but he knew the dog was coming right at him. Mason knelt down and grabbed at the mass of black as it inched by him.

Bo growled and squirmed to get free, but Mason held on. Mason could feel Bo thrashing his head. Bo's weight forced him to struggle with his balance. He slammed against a tree;

he staggered into a tangle of bushes. Mason's fight with Bo was furious, but he had the upper hand. Bo's growls quieted; he yelped.

Mason breathed heavily and continued to hold Bo tight. He stepped out from the bush, holding Bo by the head with a thick branch against his throat. The truck headlights struck Mason. The man stepped out and raised his shotgun.

"If I move, it won't be the stick you hear crack," Mason said.

A standoff.

Mason broke the silence. "Hope he doesn't whiz on your carpet."

The man lowered his gun.

"All I need from you is what's covering my back and—" Mason looked down. "Something for my feet."

The man took a while to give Mason the look over. "Come on, Bo," he replied hesitantly.

Mason loosened his grip. He wasn't sure if all of this was over, but it looked like his fight with Bo was. Bo began to slip away then quickly snapped back at Mason's face. He latched into the branch, snapping it like a dry chicken bone. Mason spun away holding a piece of branch. He swung it straight for Bo's head.

The man hollered, "Bo!"

Bo turned as Mason stopped the branch before impact. Bo ran back to the man, and Mason slipped back into the bush. He watched the man pet Bo's head then look up to see Mason was gone. "Good boy, Bo. Good boy."

They turned toward the road and the truck. Mason watched them leave staying completely still and hidden in the bush. *Son of a bitch. After all of that.* He continued watching them, hoping—praying the man would forget about the shoes.

The man stopped at the truck before getting in. He looked into the ditch. Mason shook his head and looked down at his feet. He looked back up expecting the man to be holding shoes. He was surprised to see the man hadn't moved. The man turned back toward Mason then entered his truck.

CHAPTER 6

In the past, the dawn of a new day had always been uplifting for Mason. It was the promise of something new, but not this particular morning while he walked along the side of a country road. The sun rose in front of him exposing a weary and tired man who had no clue what his next move should be.

A decision had to be made, and he worried about that. The right decision... *You have no clothes, no food, no money.* Dr. Harlow's damn warning kept pounding through his head to the point where he wandered off the shoulder and onto the road itself. A blaring horn of a semi-trailer truck was all that could break him from his trance. Even that didn't have a lasting effect. *No food... no money...* and another blast from a passing car to keep him on the shoulder.

"Fuck off, Harlow. No food, no money... What about no identity, no life?" Mason fired his arms up at the car because it was the only thing nearby he could physically blame. No Identity? What did that mean exactly? Before all of this he had a job, a house, friends; a wife. He had a driver's license, a bank account, credit cards; all the things that gave everyone an identity. But Mason had none of that now. *Shouldn't Harlow have thought of that? He gives a guy his life back, but forgets about everything that gives the guy a life.* Obviously, Dr. Harlow had no plans for Mason to be where he was right now. Not providing any of these basic necessities had probably been his plan all along. How else would he keep all of his treasures with him?

Of course, this had been exactly everyone's concern when Mason started devising his break out plan. He wondered if they were still talking about it right now, along with him going it alone. His shortsightedness was now in full view. What made things worse was the fact that there was no one else he could rely on for ideas about what to do next. How he would deal with this, and everything else that came up, would be all on Mason. They were his decisions, his victories, and his mistakes.

But there was no reason for Mason to think about failure right now. At least he was alive, and he was free. Sure he was alone but having everyone else there with him would definitely be just as confusing as it had been before. The arguments, the doubt—all negative, all fear. As long as Mason stayed positive, his decisions would drive him. He would make one, and he would act on it. They would keep him moving in one direction, even if that direction was misguided.

Misguided… That was another thing Mason had not thought about. He had never been a strategic person, and he had always got along fine just planning day-by-day. But this was a completely different matter. He was starting from scratch, like a baby fresh out of the womb. The difference was that he just ditched his mother and was giving it a go on his own. Having others around might just be exactly what he needed. Those discussions, or arguments, would lead to better decisions. Maybe that synergy was absolutely necessary to make up for what Mason lacked. Maybe his hastiness to get out of there, his first decision, was about to become his first mistake.

Jesus Christ. Is this the way to think if you expect to come out of this thing alive, again? He looked up at the road he was on, and nothing was in his way now. There were just wide open fields, and a paved path to follow. Nothing here but promise. Nothing but a clean slate. That had to be a positive thing, if he let it. It was up to him. All him. No family. No friends. No one just like him. No one to take care of him.

He stopped and stared at the long, empty road ahead. *You're dead, Mason. You're dead, Mason. You're dead.* He grabbed his head with both hands. He closed his eyes and held it still. After a moment, he let go.

He started walking again. *One step at a time.* He walked past a sign: "*Rocksbrough, population 25,000.*"

CHAPTER 7

Mason had always thought of Rocksbrough as a small town, but not so small that everyone knew what everyone else did. When he walked in at first light looking like he should be buried under six feet of dirt, he was quite sure no one knew who he was. Those watching him didn't know he was a dead man walking, and they certainly had no idea he just betrayed his savior. Mason kept walking thinking any second someone would confront him, but they only watched.

He had made the decision about what his next move would be. He knew where he was going, and where he was now was not it. This was a new part of this town, Rocksbrough Heights. Mason had never complained about what he had, but he never had enough to afford living out here. He lived where Rocksbrough started, just outside downtown. The houses he passed now were new or next to new. His house had been new when Rocksbrough was new a hundred and fifty years ago. He moved there when he found a job he couldn't find where he grew up. So basically, Mason had been a stranger here, at least in these parts. But never had he been as much a stranger as he was now.

As he walked further into town, Mason couldn't help but think of how thankful he should be for living here. This was a good place that welcomed him with opened arms and a good life. Back then, the new plant had been everything Rocksbrough needed to get it to where it was today. He remembered a lot of young people coming here for the same reason he did which made fitting in easy. He joined a gym where he met friends. He went to bars where he met Jill. They got married in Rocksbrough's United Church. The guys at the gym formed a ball team who played against teams from the town's fire department, the EMS crew, the police department, and some random guys who hadn't belonged to any groups. When he got sick, the hospital here had taken care of him the best they could. When he died… *Just how much of Rocksbrough knows what happened when I died?*

Mason stopped walking. He looked around and realized he was approaching downtown. In the distance he could see the police station. He sighed with the thought that this was one of his choices—go directly to the police. He had already made the decision not to do that, but seeing the station and knowing he could do it right then… Mason didn't know what it was, but something was fucked up with that. He shook his head and started walking again.

***

The next stop was Mason's destination in this miserable journey he had forced himself to take. He hoped it was the beginning of a new life. Maybe an extended life was a better way to put it. Either way, a life hopefully.

He knew this section of town well which wasn't nearly as manicured as Rocksbrough Heights. Forget the professional landscaping and city maintained boulevards. The properties he looked at had none of that. The people who lived here were mostly plant folks who failed to benefit from years of a thriving Rocksbrough. Houses were old, small, and mostly falling apart at the hinge. He thought it was like the rest of the town had lost interest here and moved on. But it was still occupied with a community of good people, and he had been one of them. The question was whether or not he could pick up where he left off. Would these good people see him as they did before, or would they shit all over him like they would to any other bum trying to squat in their cherished piece of the world?

Mason turned onto a small road without curbs. He stopped at the corner and took in the whole street. Not much had changed since he had last been here. The same 72 Chevy El Camino rusted away at the side of the property he stood in front of. A half built garage at a house further down stuck out in an odd location. It was an obvious afterthought that stopped construction. He started walking slowly while staring at a small rundown house on the other side of the street. It was curtainless with mail and newspapers overflowing the mailbox, but Mason saw none of that. He just saw the house he got closer to with every step, and that brought on a flood of memories.

Mason bought the house just after he started at the plant. Odd behavior for a young guy who had just rolled into town, and it definitely hadn't been what everyone else was doing. For Mason though, it had been his way of settling down, and Rocksbrough would be just as good a place as any to do that. It hadn't been much more of a house than it was now, but it had been what Mason needed most. When he had that, he needed someone to share it with; but that didn't come without a little fun first.

He remembered the main source of that fun coming from his neighbor and best friend, Reg. Reg had been different from Mason because he was married and his wife was pregnant back then, but that didn't stop these two from baseball league and pub crawls. Pub crawls often led to late night smack downs which the two of them excelled at. Of course those smackdowns required devotion to the gym which created a bonding circle, joining them at the hip. That had been until Mason met Jill.

The one thing Mason could remember best, was when he met Jill at one of the bars during a fight with another ball player who had been dating, of course, Jill. Mason won the fight which got him a drink with her and got him someone to stagger home with. That got him laid; got him breakfast, and it got him his roommate.

Mason had been a good match for Jill because he had a job and a home which meant she no longer needed either. That hadn't bothered him much then, and it still didn't. She was good for Mason because her need to do nothing gave him someone to care for which he wanted more than anything, especially now.

So Mason stood there thinking of his life with Jill in their nice, small house; in a nice, small town; until it was all ripped away with horrible news that everything would drastically change. For Mason, the change had been all about survival. He knew Jill never saw it that way though. For her, the change had been about no longer being looked after but having to return the favor and start looking after Mason. Special meals, sickness, groceries, laundry, dishes… He knew the thought of all that hadn't sat well with Jill, so she started to think outside the box—the box being the house. Even though she had physically stayed by his side, he knew she hadn't been thinking much about him.

CHAPTER 8

For most people in this part of town, it was much too early in the day for movement. Unlike Reg who opened his front door and looked outside while he held a steaming cup of coffee. He held it up to his mouth, ready to down enough to satisfy his huge appetite, when he realized his near mistake. Instead, he blew on it lightly, like a little old lady a third his size.

He heard knocking next door, then silence. He walked down the steps toward his truck. There was more knocking—louder this time. He turned but no one was there. Intending to ignore it, he moved away and tried another sip from his hot pick-me-up. Then there was pounding which was enough to catch Reg's total attention. He put his coffee down and doubled his pace to the house.

"Jill! For Christ's sake, I don't have a friggin' key," Mason yelled but not from where Reg could see him.

Reg rounded the corner. He saw a man pounding again, just short of going through. "Open the God damn door, Jill!"

"Ain't no jewels in that one, pal," Reg calmly said with a chuckle.

***

Mason breathed as though he forgot how. He looked back, saying nothing. He knew this moment would come, but he hadn't really done anything in his mind to prepare for it. He cautiously confronted his best friend with wide eyes.

Reg shook his head and laughed. "Sorry, man, but you're one lucky son of a bitch. The guy who used to live here woulda been ready to kick the shit out of—"

Mason wasn't sure what Reg was laughing at. He figured he should be shocked at seeing his dead friend. How else would he react? But no, Reg was laughing.

Reg stepped closer, and the laughing stopped. "Man, you could cut a page right out of his book." Reg's investigation continued. He snorted. "Add twenty five pounds and the boxcar build Mason had, you'd be a dead ringer."

Now Mason was the one laughing. "Dead... ringer, right?"

"Do you know Jill?" Reg relaxed. He waved his finger. "You figured you could come by and pick from what Mason left behind."

"The Reg I remember wouldn't find that funny."

"What's friggin' funny, man, is watching a guy trying to rip off an empty house. But if you know Jill—" Reg appeared confused. "How do you know my—"

Frustrated, Mason replied, "It's not that friggin' funny when the empty house is yours."

"Come on. You're trying to tell me a guy who looks like Mason, who's with a chick named Jill, just bought their house?" Reg laughed it off. "What are the friggin' odds?" He shook his head. "Jill, your wife?"

"Yeah, Reg, Jill's my wife. Where the fuck's Jill?" Mason said showing more frustration.

"Okay, let me get this straight. Now you're telling me you are Mason Bushing?" Reg laughed again. "Don't think so. I went to his funeral."

"Where's my wife, Reg?" Mason replied growing more and more frustrated.

"Don't know. Who's your wife? I haven't had the pleasure of meeting her yet. Hopefully that goes better than this." Reg turned away as if to leave. He looked back. "If you're lookin' for the Jill that used to live here, she moved," he said with a skeptic's stare.

Because of some movement at Reg's front door, Mason turned to the house. Reg's wife, Stace, looked out the door. She was just as Mason remembered. Thin, attractive; but he thought she looked tired. More tired than ever before.

Reg announced sarcastically, "Stace, look here. According to this guy, we're wakin' the dead on Maple Avenue."

Stace's eyes suddenly opened wide and stared straight at Mason. Not nearly as skeptical as Reg, she asked, "Mason?"

Mason was distracted when two young kids, Emma and Kyle, came to the door from behind her. She stepped outside, onto the porch. "Jesus Christ, Reg, does it talk? Does he ever look like Mason, Reg."

"And he sounds like Mason. And he's looking for someone named Jill. And he says he owns the place."

Completely calm now, Mason smiled at her.

"Did Mason have a brother, Stace?" Reg turned back. "Are you—"

"Hey, Skillet," Mason said.

She shook her head slowly. "Oh, no. No way." She started smiling. She looked down to see Emma beside her. "I haven't been called that in a while." She picked Emma up then looked back to Mason. "He died of cancer. You can't fake that." She took a deep breath. "Come to think of it, it wouldn't surprise me a whole lot."

Mason watched her walk down the steps. Kyle was still behind the front door. She put Emma down then started to cry, silently.

Mason noticed but made no attempt to go to her. He knew what Reg was capable of, and there was no way he intended to disturb the gentle giant.

Reg noticed Stace too. "Come on, Stace. The guy's gonna try to sell us somethin'. Watch," Reg said in an attempt to lighten the mood.

Stace chuckled slightly and stopped crying. "Yes, of course. No doubt about that," she replied while quickly wiping tears.

Mason just watched her when she looked back at him.

"He just brings back so many memories." She turned away quickly; it was no use. She covered both her eyes.

Mason said, "Shhhh, Skillet. I'm okay." He hesitated. "I came looking for Jill, not to drag you guys down with any of this."

There was an awkward silence.

Reg went to Stace; he held her. "Shit, man, you're messin' with my wife here."

Mason turned back to his house. "When did she leave?"

"They…" Stace responded but stayed in Reg's protective arms. "Moved two months ago."

Mason stood motionless. "They?"

"Hi, Uncle Mason," Kyle called from the front door.

Mason looked back and noticed Reg suddenly looking like he pissed himself.

"Hey, Kyle," Mason replied, relieved at the sight of Kyle's kindergarten smile. "What happened to your teeth?"

Kyle licked where his two front teeth were missing. "Daddy said he was gonna knock 'em out, so I did it myself."

Mason smiled at Reg who seemed to be still struggling with this. "You're a lucky kid. I've seen him do that."

Stace looked back to Mason. She picked up Emma and began walking to the house. Stace said, "Death doesn't suit ya, Mason?"

Reg shook his head. "Augh shit, Stace. Don't tell me—"

Mason looked away and noticed a blue van speeding off.

"Coffee's hot, Mason. Come get your head straight. Our

heads—" Stace said.

"Stace, what the fuck. Next you're gonna be feedin' him," Reg objected. "You're hungry right, pal?"

"Who was that?" Mason turned back sharply to Reg. "The van… Who was drivin' that van?"

Reg responded, "Christ, man. Larry the cable guy? How would I know?"

Mason was confused, but he stayed there. Beside his house. Beside Reg. Beside everything that, at least, used to be his.

"You ever see that guy? Fucker cracks me up," Reg joked but he was the only one who found it funny.

Mason didn't really hear any of what Reg just said. He was trying hard to get his head around everything.

"Okay, Mason's brother. The lady says coffee, and I know she'll be makin' eggs. If you try to sell me somethin', you're out on your ass."

CHAPTER 9

The door crept open but just a crack. Kyle peeked in then carefully entered while watching Mason shifting on his bed in a room that contained the bed, a small dresser, and not much else. He eyed some toys piled up against the dresser. It was an obvious attempt to make room for the temporary occupant. He quietly made his way over to them and started sorting through.

He looked back to Mason, out cold and oblivious to him. Kyle froze when Mason suddenly woke up to the sound of a hand slamming down on a counter.

"Damn it, Stace!" Reg's voice thundered from another room. "You're not telling me you believe that shit?"

Kyle grabbed his Huggopotamus and flew for the exit leaving the door open.

***

Mason sprung up nearly falling off the bed. His eyes grew as big as the huge buttons on Kyle's toy while he watched the rodent like kid scurry away.

"Reg, you're gonna wake him," Stace replied in a hushed voice. "And so what if I do believe him? Does that mean I'm stupid or something just because I'm not willing to take the easy way out?"

Reg calmed his tone but not his message. "Stace, it has nothing to do with a simple answer. It's just common sense. What he told us means only one thing—we're simply being fucked with."

"Well, that's not the way I see it."

"What makes you think it's even him? And with that story he's feeding us—"

"What makes you think it isn't, Reg?"

"Really? I have to answer that?"

"Reg, I know it's him. He called me Skillet. Not that he said it, but the way it came out."

Nothing was said for a second, but Mason listened anyway.

"Mason's not dead, Reg."

Mason stirred in the bed. He watched a bobble head gargoyle on Kyle's dresser in full agreement.

***

Just like Kyle's room, the kitchen Stace hurried around was small. On top of that, Reg was in her way. "And it looks to me like he's got more to worry about than whether you think he's full of shit or not," Stace said smartly as she started to organize dishes in the sink without any real purpose.

Reg looked away shaking his head.

She stopped and stared at him with obvious body language for him to move, but Reg didn't go anywhere.

She touched him on the shoulder to calm the tension. "Give him a break, Reg. Mason's a strong and smart guy. Whatever he's doing, I'm sure he's got it covered."

"Strong sure, but smart? He's just another penniless factory worker. Only difference is, he decided to leave something behind," Reg said with nothing but a jealous tone as he shifted to let Stace get by.

Stace opened the cupboard doors then stopped with a sigh. "My God, Reg. Just let him do his thing. It's not like he's fishin' to get anything from us." She turned back to see Reg take a deep breath, shake his head, and sit down at the table.

"Well, if it is him, he did get something from me. A year of my valuable sympathy." He cringed with tight lips. "I just keep feeling a hook tuggin' on my cheek, and it fuckin' hurts."

***

Great start, Mason Bushing. Wrestling with dogs, sleeping in kiddy beds, and now fighting friends. Mason continued lying on the bed with his eyes wide open. He couldn't help but second guess where he was right now. Was searching for Jill, exposing himself like this, the right first move? He couldn't see he had any other choice. Surrounding himself with family and close friends had to be the first step toward the inevitable confrontation with anyone who demanded to know what he had done and why. The problem was, he didn't have any control over what he had done, and who was going to actually believe what really happened? *The crazy doctor; a miracle drug. Yeah right.*

But of all people, these two were the ones who would at least, like Stace said, *let him do his thing.* He thought it would have been nice to have his wife on board first, by his side for all the doubters inevitably coming; but the ice was broken here, so this would have to be how it went down. It didn't matter anyway, he convinced himself. He knew things would work out. He just needed to get through the rough spots. When Jill was back by his side, everything would be just like it had been before.

Just the thought of that reunion put a smile on Mason's face, and it made him realize his decision to come here first was definitely the right one. He wondered what Jill was doing right now without him. She was a very dependent person. Her need for Mason had been strong—as strong as his need for her was now. As far as Mason could see, this was a good thing. It would bring them together; closer than they had been before. They would have a chance to rebuild what they'd lost; find a deeper love than they ever could have imagined. But now he thought she must be going through hell having lost him over a year ago with no one to turn to.

He wondered why she left the house. He always felt good about the fact he would leave her that. When dying, he knew it would be one less thing she would have to worry about. By staying, at least she would have Stace to talk things out with. He remembered them never having much of a relationship, but the loss of him should have brought them closer and given them both someone. It must have been all too much for her to handle—all the memories lingering. His death had been the end of something good in her life, and she probably needed to go somewhere else to find that type of life again. Get a fresh start, she must be thinking. He thought the same thing. It had been one of the choices he faced after the escape, but he decided to come here to pick up where he left off.

Then he remembered what Stace said. *They, moved two months ago.* He lay there while those thoughts about seeing Jill suddenly washed away with uncertainty and jealousy. Did *they* mean what he thought *they* meant? God he hoped not, but the chances were pretty good. With a year gone by, Jill would likely be with someone else who would take care of her. *Who would it be, and where did she go?* He just hoped she was still approachable, and she didn't go too far.

Mason kicked his legs over the side of the bed. He sat looking at a cardboard cutout of a manlike iguana in the corner. *Have you got a better plan yet? I'm gonna need a better plan.*

What's my next move? He looked at the overalls lying on the floor; the shoes beside them along with a stack of nicely folded pants and a shirt.

"I came here looking for Jill, and with Jill comes two things—love and money," he whispered while bending over to pick up the overalls. He stopped just before taking them. He looked at the clothes, then unfolded the shirt instead.

CHAPTER 10

Mason had fond memories of hanging out in Reg's driveway next to his old truck. It had been where they planned their workout sessions, and their nights out. It was where he and Reg were now, with empties piling up.

"We had to work on this thing all the time before I got cancer," Mason said while inspecting the truck for any new wear. "Looks like it's holding up better than I am." He looked to Reg. "Or you for that matter."

Reg curled his lip and gave his belly a friendly tap. "Something's gotta give at some point."

"When a gasket blows," Mason said with a cautionary smile.

"You tryin' to tell me something, buddy?"

"Nothin' I'm sure you don't already know."

Mason watched Reg look down at his stomach for a closer

inspection. "Maybe we should dust off the iron." He looked back up at Mason. "Judging by the fit of that shirt, you're going the other way. We could both use a boost." He smiled and took a drink.

Mason joined him and shifted in the shirt that floated on him. He looked at the bottle while his mouthful was going down. "I can't stop counting the things I've missed out on," he said. "So you just stopped lifting?"

"Haven't moved an ounce since cancer threw you that left hook." He gave Mason a suspicious look. "You know, I should be really pissed. You put us both through—"

Mason saw Stace at the door. "Clock's set for six thirty, Reg."

"I know, baby, but this guy's been, *dead,* for over a year. You convinced me it's him, now I'll suffer," Reg said. He took a long swig from his beer.

"Use the fryin' pan on him," Mason said with a subtle smile. "Just not on me again."

"Well, do what ya want, but there's gonna be a price," Stace said.

Mason watched her starting to close the door. Reg held up his beer. Mason did the same.

"That's one bill I can pay right now," Reg said with a confident beer chug that emptied it. He wasted no time getting another.

Stace gave him a, *your choice,* look as the door closed.

Mason smiled, nodded, and took a drink. He looked toward his house. "It's good to be back, man, but either way, the struggle. When I woke up, I thought I was finally gettin' a break." He took another drink. "But judging by what it took to get here and then finding out Jill's gone. I don't know… Is the guy she's with someone who can actually take care of her?" Mason took a second to think about that. "Where is she, Reg?"

Reg drank from a fresh bottle. He walked across the driveway toward some bushes.

"Do you know?" Mason watched Reg then turned away when Reg started to urinate.

"Just forget her, Mason."

"Forget her. Shit, man, she's my wife. Would you forget Stace? If nothin' else, at least I've got love."

Reg didn't answer. He walked past Mason without saying anything, struggling to do up his zipper while he held on to his beer. "How did you fake the cancer thing anyway? Some accident or murder sure, but cancer?"

"Reg, shit, man. How many times until you believe me. I didn't fake anything."

Reg glanced at him. Mason knew what he was thinking. *You weren't born yesterday, right, but you know I'm no liar too.*

Mason looked away. "It's not you I have to convince anyway." He shook his head. "Where is she, Reg? I want to see my wife." He took another drink and looked Reg straight in the eye. "I just want my life back."

"Shit, man, you don't want to go there."

Mason stared him down.

"Do you?" Reg waited for an answer, but Mason kept

staring. "Really?" He rushed to the case of beer. "Here, buddy, have another." He looked back to Mason with a fresh bottle.

Mason finished his beer. He ignored Reg's offer and put his empty with the others.

Reg shook his head and put the beer back in the case. "Okay, Okay. I'll play the game. Your crazy doctor story sucks, but an insurance scam works for me." He stood up, reached into his pocket and held up his keys.

Mason turned back with question marks for eyeballs. "Insur—" Mason suddenly froze. His mind spun.

"Just for the record, I told you to forget her." Reg opened the driver's door. "Door's open, buddy. Let's go see how the dark side lives." Reg started the truck with a loud rev. He punched it two more times to get Mason going.

Mason got in, sat down, and stared blankly out the window. He instinctively started to close the door. The truck surged.

***

Stace watched from the kitchen window as the truck spit up rocks on its way out of the driveway.

CHAPTER 11

"Rocksbrough Heights" highlighted the elaborately landscaped sign Mason stared at as they turned off the main road into a new subdivision. Mason had not spent much time out here in the past. Sure, he had seen it before. He had driven out here with Jill to see the houses; but it hadn't been where he, or where anyone he cared about, came from. So basically, he had stayed away. There had been a lot of talk about this place when it was being developed, but any conversation about it on Maple Avenue hadn't involved anyone suggesting they would move there. Those people were blue collar; the people coming here were executive. The houses being built were estates, and Mason knew they weren't being built for him.

Jill was the same—at least back then, when she had been with Mason. Did some guy she hooked up with change all that, or was it the money? The insurance policy. How much was that for? He couldn't remember. He hadn't been involved that much with it. *Just sign here,* she said, and Mason did.

He sighed and tried to blink the thought of money away. "She's not with anyone I know if they're campin' out here," he said in an otherwise silent truck cab. He looked back out the window at luxury.

"Hey, brother, you died, she cashed. Wasn't that the plan?" Mason caught Reg's skeptical look. "Didn't expect her to spend it, right?"

Mason knew Reg was looking for a reaction, but he ignored him. He kept watching what passed in front of him: attached three car garages, stone entrances, tiled rooftops, pillars, arches, circular driveways. Mason's dreams of success had never stretched as far as what he was witnessing.

"I know you had an awesome policy, man, but I never woulda guessed you were the type to scam it. I just hope you guys studied the shit out of your playbook."

Mason gave Reg a curious glance, but he wasn't really listening to him. He was preoccupied trying to take all this in. *Did I really sign on to a policy worth this much? And this is what she did with it?* Mason couldn't believe he actually set himself up to be worth way more dead than alive. He also couldn't believe he completely forgot about it.

They slowly drove by a large house with a new convertible Mustang in the driveway. Mason stared at it. They continued down the street, but Mason never looked away from the house.

Reg started tapping the steering wheel. Mason heard it, but he didn't react.

"That's it, right?" Mason said almost hypnotically.

"Not what you expected?"

Mason looked straight ahead. "Expectations change. Let's do it."

"Do what?" The truck stopped. "You did expect something like this, right?" There was still nothing from Mason. "Mason, hey."

Reg's hand waived in front of Mason's face.

"You guys are cookin' up something. Right, Mason?"

Mason continued staring straight ahead. "Nothing that's on my menu," he said. "It's time to talk to the chef."

"Well I don't remember Jill being much into cooking, but yeah, let's do that. Just in case things weren't crazy enough," Reg mumbled.

Mason started to feel nervous as the truck turned around and stopped in front of the large house. He got out. He stopped before crossing the street. He looked at the house again then slowly made his way across. He stopped in the driveway, beside the car. He took a quick look inside then back to the house. Mason started walking again, focused on the elaborate pillared and peaked entrance.

He knocked loudly on the front door. Without giving much time for anyone to answer, he knocked again.

Mason noticed the blinds in the front window open. Dressed in a t-shirt and boxers, the guy standing on the other side of the window had visible frustration lines on his face, even from where Mason was standing.

Mason banged. The door swung open.

"Who's the fucked up loser bangin' my door down at this time?"

It was hardly the way to greet a guest at his front door, but by the looks of this guy, to him it was more than appropriate. "I'm lookin' for Jill," Mason said in a relatively calm voice.

The guy looked beyond Mason. "Who the fuck is this?" Frustration was now confusion—a deadly combination.

"Who do ya think he is? Looks like your bank roll's over," Reg answered.

The guy looked back to Mason.

Mason said, "The next time I ask won't be with words." Now he knew Reg was behind him. He'd been in the situation with Reg many times before, and it never went well, for the other guy anyway.

The guy laughed, but judging by the look on his face, he wasn't finding any of this funny. "Fuck you," he replied. "You assholes think I'm fuckin' stupid?"

There was a noise from behind him. He looked back and took a second to think this through. Mason stayed calm, but he was surprised a bit. Out of nowhere, this guy's aggressive tone suddenly changed.

"Listen, you fuckups just caught a huge break. I'm going to consider this a bad dream so fuckin' beat it." He began to close the door.

Mason saw Jill appear from behind him. "Mason?"

Mason smiled. "Yeah, Jill. Who said the only sure thing in life is death and—"

She was stunned. "No way."

"I'm not dead, Jill."

"And you're not Mason either."

Mason had hoped for a better reaction, but this is exactly what he figured would happen. As soon as they turned into Rocksbrough Heights, all his thoughts about a wonderful reunion with Jill suddenly began to turn on him.

He looked away, unsure how to react. "Thought you'd be thrilled."

"Thrilled, about what?" Jill snapped back. "Seeing some guy who looks like my dead husband tryin' to scam me in the middle of the night?" She shook her head.

"It's me, Jill."

"It's me, Jill," the guy mimicked. "You've got to be fucking kiddin' me."

Mason stayed put as Jill pulled the guy into the house. "Close the door, Tom."

He started to, but Mason stopped it. "I thought we were in love."

She snapped back, relieved. "Well there you go. Mason never had a clue about love."

Mason realized right then he also never had a clue about the woman he married.

"Fuck this," Tom said. He stepped out of the house and confronted Mason. "You guys think you're gonna pull some shit on us. Think again."

Suddenly, Mason was up against the wall with Tom inches from him. Mason didn't react. He was here for Jill, and Tom was just an obstruction.

"Tom, don't," Jill said with sudden urgency. She stared hard at Mason. "I know you're not Mason. Just a good replica."

Tom moved away with a small push.

Jill stepped out from the house. Mason watched her look to the driveway.

"Reg." She shook her head, unimpressed. "You just can't take the fact that I cashed in, and you're still walkin' with your head down lookin' for loose change."

Mason watched Reg walk toward the front door.

"Fuck you, Jill. You're just a lazy bitch." He turned to Mason. "Come on, man. Crazy doc or fearless scam, either way, she's not buyin' it."

Tom turned suddenly to Reg. "You callin' my woman a bitch?"

"Sure am, Tommy, and over the past year, that's pretty much a compliment I'd say." Reg stood his ground.

"Believe what you want, Jill, but I'm not feedin' worms. Some crazy doctor had another idea," Mason said trying for an explanation.

Tom sarcastically said, "Really, what happened?"

Mason continued but he only talked to Jill. "He locked me up with psychos—a lab rat for his crazy experiments."

Tom started to laugh. Mason noticed Tom starting to pace with small steps. *His frustration's building–not good.*

Mason continued, "Picked the wrong guy for that."

Tom laughed again, hysterically now. "You said psycho, right?"

Reg turned away, embarrassed.

Jill stared at Mason. "You're fuckin' weird, man."

Mason was frustrated, surrounded in a sea of doubt. "You know it's me, Jill, but believe what you want. Just give me some of my money since I've got nothin'. Not even a dime."

Tom stopped pacing and spun around shaking his head.

"Then I'll leave," Mason said.

Tom stopped laughing. "You're gonna be leavin', pal, but no money is." Tom lunged at Mason. Again he was in Mason's face, but Mason wasn't nearly as relaxed this time.

Jill shouted, "Tom, don't. You'll wake up everyone."

"What's wrong, Jill?" Reg said then upped the volume. "The neighbors don't party?"

Mason saw Jill stare daggers at Reg. He stumbled a bit to clear himself from Tom's face.

"That's right you fuckin' idiot. Maybe in your shithole neighborhood everyone thinks this stuff is entertainment. Here they don't."

Mason regained his balance. It was now at the point where Tom's obstruction had to be dealt with. He came up with a punch to the side of Tom's face.

Tom surged at Mason again. They landed on the walkway then into the garden. Mason rolled on top and punched him again. He got onto his feet and jumped back a short distance. His arms were at his side, but he was ready to fight.

Tom slowly got up. He took a shaky step toward Mason.

Jill screamed, "Tom, leave it alone! Just come back."

Tom looked back to Jill then stepped closer. Mason was ready and punched again connecting with Tom's nose. Blood poured.

"You know it's me. Jill," Mason growled with his frustration building that was obviously going to be taken out on this guy in front of him.

"Tom, stop. He's stronger than you. Stop."

Mason threw another shot sending Tom to the ground. He looked up at Jill. "You know it's me," he said while preparing for his next assault.

Tom tried to get up. Mason kicked him. "You want me to stop? Get some cash." He yelled, "How much did ya get, Jill? Get me some fuckin' money."

Mason watched Jill look back into the house then she started to cry. "You know it's fuckin' me." Mason was totally raged now. He kicked Tom again, and again.

"Mason, I don't like the guest list," Reg said right next to Mason.

Mason paid no attention to Reg. He only looked at Jill. "You got insurance on him too? Might be tough claiming twice," he shouted followed by another round of relentless attacks.

"Mason, stop!" she screamed then ran back into the house.

Mason stopped the attack. Jill's acknowledgment that she knew it was him was enough. He snapped back to Jill, but she was gone. He hovered over top of Tom who fought for his breath.

Reg came up from behind Mason again. "He's done, Mason. I think Jill's right on this one, pal. Anything else and there's probably gonna be cops joining in."

Mason was focused back on Tom. "They're gonna have to stand in line." He lined up his leg for another beating but hesitated. "Take the truck and wait around the corner."

Reg said, "Okay, man."

Mason walked around then toward the front door. He looked back at Tom.

Jill rushed out from the house. "Here, take it. Just leave him alone." Money was almost falling from her hands.

"Why, Jill? You think he deserves better? You guys live off my misfortune, and he deserves better?"

Mason noticed car lights coming slowly down the street. He looked at the money, then to her. "I thought you loved me."

Jill saw the car too. She pushed the money at Mason and ran to Tom.

Mason watched her quickly trying to get him moving. He stood there then noticed the car lights getting closer. It was a cop. He started running, in the direction Reg left.

Mason passed Reg sitting in his truck. It roared to a start, but Mason kept running. He ran hard, but he knew a cop was closing in. Mason made a move to cross the street, but that turned out to be his mistake. He stumbled over a curb.

He was grabbed by the cop. As the cop tried to pull

Mason down, Mason threw his elbow back, catching the cop in the mouth.

"You fuckin' bastard," the cop moaned.

Mason hit the ground hard with the cop on top of him. He took two punches to the head, then a knee to the ribs. He rolled away and was hit by the lights from the police car. The cop kneed him again. Mason looked up at him, moaning. The cop moved his tongue and spit a tooth.

Mason was suddenly being hauled to his feet by another cop, or two—he didn't know. He was forced against the car, and his head slammed down sideways on the trunk. He felt his wrists being promptly cuffed behind his back.

He couldn't get away now. He breathed heavily but tried to calm himself while Reg drove by, slowly.

PART II

"DEATH, WAS MY ONLY MISTAKE."

CHAPTER 12

Mason's days of freedom were extremely short lived and drastically different from what he had envisioned. Months and months of planning his great escape turned into this— one day of liberty. Other than getting away from Dr. Harlow, this whole thing couldn't have strayed farther off his path back to reality. It was a new start that turned out to be nothing more than being locked up again.

Now he sat at a single table with a face that showed the events from the night before. He was alone and forced to stare at nothing because there was nothing in the room except him, the table, and another chair. Could this place be any more like a cheap movie set? Even a fake mirror took up most of one wall. He huffed and shook his head. That little movement caused him to grab his side, wincing in pain. He wanted to look at himself in the mirror, but he resisted. He didn't want to give the pricks on the other side the pleasure of seeing his brutally beaten up face. Any minute now, he expected a cop, no two cops, to mosey on in and start doing the same old song and dance. *Naw, even this place has to be more advanced than that.* He softly touched his swollen shut eye then reluctantly looked closely at himself in the mirror.

Suddenly, the door swung open. Someone was pushed into the room by a uniformed officer. "Take a seat, hero," the officer commanded then pulled the door shut leaving an echo ringing and Mason alone with who knows who.

"Fuck you, ya big dick. Or is that too much of a compliment?" the guy said with the same little respect he was just given.

Mason watched him try the handle.

It was locked. He kicked it. "Fuckin' asshole." He spun around. "Oh, another bad guy."

Mason kept eye contact with this intruder now circling the table, staring intensely at him.

"They better not make us share beds. You're too fuckin' ugly."

Mason didn't move. At first he didn't know what to make of this. Two guys interrogated at the same time? Not likely. Mason wanted to get up when the guy stopped directly in front of him, but he didn't. He looked away to break the stare down.

The guy leaned forward for a closer look. "Buddy, that face seriously needs a makeover. The boys in blue must have brought you in the back door."

Mason said nothing, but he looked up. He shook his head, unimpressed. *They must have banged around some heads other than mine to come up with this.*

"So you're who they're all fucked up about out there." The guy said, "Nice scam, man." He took a seat. "Not gonna work though."

Mason got up. He mumbled, "What the fuck is this?" He tried the door knowing it would get him nowhere.

"It's locked. Like we got somewhere to go," the guy said.

Mason took a deep breath and leaned back against the door. He stroked his eyebrows remembering quickly the pain. He clinched his lips and opened his one working eye as wide as it would allow.

The guy continued, "See, the part about your wife with the guy ya almost killed. You shouldn't have done that. It's too obvious."

Mason started to walk around the room. *How am I going to get these jokers to believe me?*

"And the crazy doctor thing. You think anyone's gonna believe that?"

Mason stopped walking. He looked back at the guy. *That's simple. I'm not.*

***

A supervisor stood with two police officers who sat at a table. They faced a window looking into the interrogation room. The supervisor watched, entertained like it was his favorite ball team on a big screen projector, but he was concerned just the same. "Looks like we've got Warren back. They say change is good. I'm not so sure." He watched Warren turn with his chair to face Mason. "He just needs to stay focused on the prize." He coached Warren with his eyes. He might as well have been watching his favorite power hitter step up to the plate with the bases loaded.

"Let me help you out here, pal. A little con to con advice," Warren said.

The supervisor watched him begin to work out a plan, thinking with his hands.

"I'm not really sure what way you're trying to go with this, but whatever you do—"

The supervisor tapped his finger hard on the table between the two cops. "Are you guys taking notes?" He focused on Warren's performance. "You're watching a pro here. Any second this bimbo's gonna crack. I'm telling ya, every time—as soon as they start to talk, all the sugar coated details come pouring out." He left the table and anxiously got closer to the window.

***

Mason continued pacing, oblivious to the intruder's rambling. He took short, rapid breaths. He clinched his teeth that barely showed through his tight lips.

The guy continued, "You gotta swing their attention away from—"

Mason fired a piercing stare straight at the mirror. "Do you guys think I'm fuckin' stupid? The story's not gonna change." He looked to the guy then back. "It's the only one I've got. I am Mason Bushing. I'm not dead." Mason stormed toward him. "If you don't believe me, go dig me up. I won't be there. I'm standing right in front of you," he said aggressively, inches from the guy's face.

The guy bolted up from the chair. He pushed Mason back, but Mason held his ground. "And I'm Detective Warren Fillmore. I don't think you're dead, Mason fucking Bushing. I think you're lying." Warren kept his stare locked on Mason.

Mason didn't back away, but he didn't take it any further.

"Think about what you went through last night. Think about the way you look now. Think about how this will turn out if you keep going down this road," Warren said.

Mason didn't flinch, but Warren breathed hard distracting Mason. It broke the stare down.

Warren eased away and headed for the door. "It's time you start worrying about whether that guy presses charges."

Mason replied, "The same guy who's doin' my wife and spendin' all my cash? And she's signin' the cheques. Is that what your wife would do?"

Warren stopped dead, but Mason wasn't sure why. Warren looked down in total silence then took a deep breath. He spun around with flared nostrils. Warren attacked. "You mean my *dead* wife?"

Mason ducked, but Warren was all over him. His hands were in his face. Mason slammed up against the wall.

"You're playin' a game with death, and it's the only God damn thing I can think about," Warren shouted, spit flying inches between them.

Mason saw the door fly open. Officers poured in. Warren was pulled away leaving Mason shocked and overwhelmed.

Warren brushed everyone off; he composed himself. He started to leave but stopped.

Mason watched him stare down the supervisor.

"For whatever reason that I can't figure out for the life of me, some asshole thought it would be fuckin' hilarious to put me on a case with some low life on a death wish."

Suddenly, Mason was his center of attention again.

"Well believe me Mason Bushing, I'm going to find out whatever shit it is you're up to which will leave you with only one thing–*fucked*." He turned back to the door. "Book him on assaulting a cop."

Mason said, "Book who? Remember, I'm dead." He steadied himself, ready for another attack.

At the door, Warren turned back. "And fraud. Insurance fraud." He left, pushing past the supervisor.

Mason sighed with relief when everyone started to leave. Everyone except one cop. He smiled at Mason, showing him his missing tooth.

CHAPTER 13

Warren sat in an armchair, alone in the dark. He stared at a picture of Linda that was placed on a table among other cherished items. It glowed, highlighting it from the other objects that were dull, blurry, and greyed out because of the lack of light. This is exactly the way Warren wanted to remember her: beautiful, elegant, picture perfect. She had always been his answer when things got out of control. She brought him back; she led him to the place where everything made sense again. Because he was a cop, he needed that. Now that she was gone, this picture was all he had, so its angelic glow was just how he needed it to be.

It wasn't just the image of her that made him look at nothing else in the room. He also got a wonderful feeling of her being right there with him. If he looked away, the feeling was instantly gone. After he did that a few times, he became nervous about losing her again and again. That trapped him into staring at her, but he was okay with that. He knew he was physically alone and without her, but magically, they were together because of that picture.

The phone suddenly rang breaking Warren away. He was disoriented at first; not able to locate the phone, but it was ringing right beside him. He picked up a handset. Before he got it to his ear, he heard the roaring sound of strong wind or possibly highway traffic. He looked at the handset then he heard a faint voice.

"Warren. Warren, are you there?"

The voice was hardly audible but unmistakably Linda. He quickly slammed the phone to his ear.

"Warren. Please, Warren, answer."

"Linda?" He pulled the phone back while shaking his head to get rid of the illusion.

"Warren, oh my God, Warren honey, thank God it's you."

He slowly repositioned the phone to his ear. He listened intently but said nothing. Quickly, he lost confidence in the credibility of the caller.

"Warren, are you there? Please talk to me, Warren. Please."

"If I talk, will it add to your cheap thrill or give you a complete source of insane pleasure?" Warren said.

"Warren, you have to believe me. I'm not dead. I can explain it all later, but you have to come and get me."

"Okay, where? I'll send the whole force," he said sarcastically, ready to hang up.

"Warren, it's me. Please believe it's me. Come for me, Warren, before they do."

"Oh, they now? Who's coming for you?"

"They're not coming for me, they're coming after me."

"Okay fine, they're coming after you. Then tell me who's coming after you, and where I should come to get you. And by the way, who you are would be good too."

"You don't believe it's me, Warren? Tell me you believe me."

Warren didn't answer. It sounded like Linda. He wanted to believe it was her. *Oh, God, I want to believe it;* but he knew better.

"Ahhh, best bet here would be no, it's not you, Linda."

Another voice took over. It was a male voice. "Warren, for Christ's sake. Just tell her you believe it's her just like you want to believe it's her. Just tell her you believe she's not dead, just like you believe Mason Bushing is not dead."

The voice went silent. Warren didn't respond. He just sat, thinking, with the phone to his ear.

"Or, you could tell her you think she's a *liar.*"

Fucking Mason Bushing. "Son of a bitch. How did you get out?" Suddenly, the voice was gone as well as the wind, or traffic, or whatever. There was only dead air now—silence on the phone, and silence in his house.

I don't think you're dead, Mason. I think you're lying.

Suddenly, he jolted forward in his chair and his eyes popped open, wide awake. The lights were on in the room. The phone sat on the table beside him untouched. Linda's picture was on the table, but it wasn't glowing. Everything was fine, just as it always had been. The only thing wrong was Warren—broken beyond repair.

There had been a time, though, when Warren hadn't been broken. In fact, back then he didn't have a clue what a broken soul was. This had been when he was in love with the only woman who could see inside him. Past the image he had painted on for his detective role. Past the tough guy that needed to take over when he left here each day for work. Linda knew who Warren really was, and that guy was the same guy who had a smudge of belief in Mason's story. Why he thought that, Warren didn't know. But Linda was gone now, and so was that guy. Mason would have to deal with the other Detective Warren Fillmore. The question was whether or not Warren could handle that. Nobody else would see any difference, but Warren already struggled with how he would let this side of himself become all of him.

Maybe Linda was just his catalyst for change. Had she been in his life just to set it up? He would have to take over now and make it complete, but that wasn't likely going to happen. For as long as Warren could remember, he had always been the detective guy. Only Linda had made him realize there was someone else inside. But with Linda gone, that Warren might just as well go back into hiding, because really, what good was he now? Or maybe Mason was the next step—the guy who says he's risen from the dead. Is he Warren's hope for a new beginning?

Warren shook himself out of the daydream. *Holy fuck, man.*

Get a grip of yourself. It's just another case. He looked around his living room that was decorated with high end furniture, designer drapery; an antique area rug over honey brown oak hardwood. Other than the state of the art entertainment system, nothing in here screamed Warren the Detective, so eventually it would have to go.

For now though, Warren had a case to solve which, on the surface, seemed fairly cut-and-dry. This guy was scammin' an insurance payout, plain and simple except for one thing. If it was Linda saying this, he would believe her, so why would he think Mason was lying? *Ahh, I know the answer to that. Because he's not Linda. He had never seen Linda. He had nothing in common with Linda. He had never even crossed paths with Linda.* So that made it fine? Given the same situation, he would believe Linda but not Mason? He shook his head and found himself staring at the picture again. Her look told him she disagreed. He looked away. *Just process the case, and get it over with.*

He looked at his wrist watch—3:23. He considered getting up and going to his bedroom, but there was a certain comfort here surrounded by all the things that reminded him of Linda. So he didn't move. He sat back in his chair and closed his eyes, but they didn't stay that way.

CHAPTER 14

In the past, Mason always knew of the Rocksbrough Police Department as a modern structure with smoked glass windows, a canopied entrance, and a landscaped courtyard; but he knew now this was just a makeover for the real building it covered. He never knew this was one of the first buildings built in Rocksbrough, and Mason was currently being detained close to where the first footings were poured. Dark, damp, and musty were all that could be expected down here. It was the perfect place for the town's liars, thieves, con artists, and criminals.

Mason lay curled up on the cot with no blanket and no pillow. The cell he occupied was bigger than eight by ten, but only because it was supposed to hold two. Mason was told when the door was locked that he should consider himself lucky because he was the only bad guy in Rocksbrough today, and if his luck held, he'd be able to take a shit in private.

He knew his face was recovering because he could see a slit of life from the eye that had been totally shut. He heard commotion, so he turned to a wall of bars. He had a clear view from his unharmed eye.

Warren arrogantly entered the detainment area with someone else behind him. *Great, this detective guy again; and look at that, he brought backup.* From what Mason could tell though, the sidekick wasn't another tough cop; but he was obviously there for Mason, so that automatically made him the enemy too. *Two against one; three if you consider the dick on desk duty. Pretty good odds against a guy who's already facing a standing eight count.*

Warren approached the young cop at the duty desk. "Wake up ya lyin' bastard," he said and took a key.

Mason watched the young cop jolt up. He tucked away his phone and pretended to be heavy into paperwork.

"Story's original. I'll give him that much," Warren said to the guy with him. Warren continued straight to Mason's cell and shook the bars before inserting the key in the door. "I said wake up. Doctor's here to check your vitals. Prove ya still got some." He slid the door wide open. It came to a crashing stop. "And I wouldn't advise any smart ass moves or wise cracks. I'm a cranky bastard today with very little sleep."

Mason jumped off the cot and slid the door shut. "No doctors." He held the door closed the best he could. "You assholes can have as much of me as you want, but get the lunatic out of here," he demanded.

Warren looked at the doctor. "Wise fuck for a dead guy." He sent Mason a piercing stare. "Normally I'm all for removing the lunatics, Mason, but in your case, we'll make an exception."

Mason didn't resist when Warren slid the door back open, softly.

"Let's try this again, and show some respect this time. Trust me, Dr. Nichols here, he'll be gentle." He looked at Dr. Nichols. "If you find anything broken, doc, break it again. Just call when you're done."

Mason braced himself for a showdown with Dr. Nichols now standing in the cell doorway. "There's no way you're touchin' me. Tell Harlow I'm all locked up again. He'll be proud of himself."

Dr. Nichols looked confused. "Doctor Harlow?"

Mason saw the young cop, beyond Dr. Nichols, shift in his chair; but Mason didn't pay much attention to him.

Dr. Nichols said, "Doctor Henry Harlow?" He shook his head and chuckled. "There's only one thing I know about Henry Harlow, Mason. It's called Purify." He looked away and giggled again. "Notice I left out the doctor part?"

Mason still watched the young cop as he took a phone from the desk, but really, Mason was only paying attention to Dr. Nichols.

"And if you think I've got anything to do with that story, well, I'll need to book some more time to show you my credentials." Dr. Nichols looked away from Mason and back to Warren.

Mason followed his glance. By the look on Warren's face, he didn't have a clue what Dr. Nichols was talking about. He was definitely listening though.

"No, Mason, I just need to see how you're holding up. If you're holding up," Dr. Nichols said, dismissing his last sentence as a joke with a snicker.

Mason scanned back to the young cop who was hammering a text message into the phone. It was something that caught Mason's attention, but it wasn't big enough to keep it. Suddenly, the young cop left.

"Christ, Warren, when are you guys gonna learn that humans do eventually break? You can call us in to fix the damage, but man…"

Mason didn't give the young cop a second thought because Dr. Nichols stood right in front of him scratching his head. He looked Mason up and down.

"So, Mason, tell me where it hurts the most if you can actually pinpoint something in this mess." He looked back to Warren with a disgusted look.

Mason looked around frantically. "Bastards. Save my life with some miracle drug. Is that what you call fix the damage? Then what do you do? Fuckin' lock me up." He continued to search like a cornered animal with nowhere to go.

Dr. Nichols took a step closer. "You look pretty roughed up, Mason. You must be able to tell me what to concentrate on."

Mason ignored the comment. He didn't care about the pain surging through his body. He only looked for a way out.

Dr. Nichols got close enough to check out the bruises on his face. He checked his eyes—at least the one he could get a quick look at with his pencil flashlight. "You know what Purify is, right?" He tried to check his ribs.

Mason pushed him away and jumped on top of the bed. "I went in there dead, and that's the only way you'll take me back."

Dr. Nichols stepped back as if not to frighten the terrified. "A fantasy drug's not going to help you. What exactly are you on, Mason? What do you need?" Dr. Nichols got closer again. "We can get it for you. Did you know that? If it's going to help, Mason, that's what we'll do." He waited for a response. "Come on, Mason. Just tell me what you need, and everything will be much better. You know the feeling I'm talking about, right, Mason?"

Mason backed up more, but the wall stopped him "You know I'm on Purify, but it's the last thing I need. What I need is a bed without a lock."

Dr. Nichols held out his hand. "Well, that story is exactly what's gonna keep you here."

He was too close now. Mason dodged him and went for the door. He slammed against the side of it which knocked him off balance. He got out for a few steps but no further.

Mason went down, hard. He squirmed on the ground, not sure what hit him until Warren picked him up like a bag of trash and slammed him against the bars.

Mason groaned in agony. He struggled to get away from Warren's grip holding his face. He felt his neck crack when Warren wrenched his head to be sure there was direct eye contact.

"I didn't hear any starting pistol go off."

Mason couldn't move, and Warren's cold stare sunk in.

"You must have forgot the part I said about little sleep."

Mason couldn't react as Warren pulled him from the bars and literally threw him back into the cell.

"Did you really think you were gonna do some dine-n-dash from the deepest hole of the town's police department?" Warren's voice thundered, echoing off the cinder block walls. "Damn, Mason, start putting a little brain power into it all; or did we fuck that up too much?" He slammed his hand against the bars adding to the echo.

Dr. Nichols was hovering over Mason now, trying to help him up. "He's right, Mason. You've got to think about the things you're doing and saying. The myth about Purify is not going to cover up an insurance scam." He noticed a bump on Mason's hip. He examined it with some, but very little, resistance from Mason. Instead, Mason twisted his head a bit to be sure nothing broke.

He looked up to see Warren standing impatiently at the door holding the key. "What the hell, doc. You keep saying Purify. How about you bring me up to speed on that one since I'm not really in the mood for guessing games."

Mason felt Dr. Nichol's hand gently pat his shoulder.

"Mason knows."

Mason looked back to him. Dr. Nichols smiled with a hand gesture that was intended to give Mason the stage.

"Tell him about Doctor Harlow and his immortality theory, Mason. The crazy military scientist whose drug had been turned down for grants over and over, so he went underground with a community of followers supporting him." He paused with a head tilt—another gesture of encouragement. "Tell him about his secret laboratory where he works on dead people. People just like you, Mason." He nodded with his eyes popping.

Mason could barely stand, but he did anyway despite everything telling him to stay down. If there was any chance for another break, he would take it; but physically, he was done. He collapsed on the bed.

"Mason also knows Doctor Harlow's not running any underground experiment. He's not about to rid the world of disease. Instead, he's dead." Dr. Nichols hovered over top of Mason. "Did you know that, Mason? Did you know your Doctor Henry Harlow is actually dead?"

Did you know you don't know shit? Mason curled up, trying to protect himself from Dr. Nichols—a threat that wasn't really there.

Mason relaxed a bit when Dr. Nichols turned back to Warren.

"It was supposed to take a living body into a comatose state. Then repair it, totally purifying the immune system to create a body that would never become infected with any disease again." Dr. Nichols left Mason on the bed and began to gather up his stuff. "Great idea, but really, who in this day and age can develop the balance between biology, chemistry, and physics to give us a working model of that?"

Mason watched him shake his head at the thought of that

and walk toward the door.

"Your prisoner's fine, Warren. He's just a good liar. I think you might have banged up his hip though."

Mason sighed when Dr. Nichols started to leave. He rubbed the bump. He hadn't noticed anything like this before, but sure enough, something was not right. He tried the other side to see if it was the same. It wasn't. He twisted the best he could to try and see it.

"Your story goes back twenty years, Mason. It's not new to anyone."

Mason looked up as Dr. Nichols passed Warren with a sarcastic smile.

"Except, maybe a cop." He stopped and touched Warren on the shoulder. "Sorry, Detective." He smiled and continued to leave.

Mason's eyes were on Warren who was watching Dr. Nichols go. Then he glanced at Mason. Warren scratched his head then slammed the door shut.

Mason forgot him as soon as the threat was gone. He went back to examining the bump.

CHAPTER 15

Warren wasn't like most of the cops working the beat in Rocksbrough. He always thought they much preferred writing traffic violations from the comfort of their cruiser's front seat than chasing down violent criminals who threaten the town's innocence. It wasn't that they didn't care about their oath to protect the people, it was the extra twenty plus pounds around their waist that simply got in the way.

Warren was in the gym finishing up his daily adrenaline fix. He was pretty much the leader of a small group that did the department's calendar proud every year. When these guys weren't hammering it out with the town's frequent offenders, they were in the PD Gym, grinding on iron for a better pump.

"Forty eight," he groaned because the last three hurt the most. "Forty nine," he said, strained behind clenched teeth.

"Fifty." He concluded the set with a power boost that caused him to grab on to the twenty pound iron slab lying on his chest. He sat straight up on the sloped sit up bench and tossed the slab to the side. It crashed hard on the rubber floor with a muffled clang. He watched it settle quickly, but he didn't take his eyes off it. He reached down for a soaked towel. He wiped the hard earned sweat from his face, breaking the stare down with a silent piece of iron.

He sat with his feet anchored, and he didn't move. Even though he seemed content that he was getting back to his daily routine, there was a strong message in his eyes that something was still very wrong. Of course it was because of Linda being gone, but that was only partially the reason. All day he thought about how he had acted with Mason first thing this morning in the detainment room. Showing his authority and demanding control of the situation wasn't eating away at him. It was his over the top aggression; the way he handled Mason when he had made a run for it that caused this turning feeling in his gut.

Really, where would have Mason gone? He could have just watched him run around in circles, but no, he had to do it his tough guy way. It was like he was brain dead from testosterone overload. This was not any different than the way Warren would have handled it when he had been on his own in the past, but he was never that way when he had been with Linda. She tamed him; had taken the beast away, but why couldn't he do that by himself? Why did he need Linda to bring out that other Warren, and why did he have to lose her to realize this was his biggest problem?

He wiped sweat again from his face and detached himself from the bench. Maybe he was just tired—no sleep from last night. He shook his head. This Warren didn't act any different with or without sleep. He acted on impulse, an instant reaction to control the situation at hand. Somehow, he was going to have to find a way to get the same result without the same aggression. Really, it shouldn't be that hard. Linda brought it out in him, so he should be able to figure it out for himself. *Just try, man. Conscious effort kinda stuff.*

He looked around the room thinking this was probably not the best place for him to be with these conflicting soft thoughts. He looked down at the slab he just tossed. *Next time we'll go without the supersize effect. Who knows, it might make a difference.* He twitched his forehead, got up, and headed for the door.

As soon as Warren stepped into the hallway, he felt uncomfortable. The gym was a good place for him because he was surrounded with others like him, and they were all preoccupied with their own hard body agenda. Outside of there it was like a stage, even though there was no one anywhere near him at the time. He always felt eyes watching him. Maybe he came back too early, and people around really were eying him down wondering how he was getting by? Maybe he just had himself up on this pedestal because his loss allowed that to make sense. Regardless, the feeling put him on a direct course to his office hoping no one would stop him with that dreaded, *how are you, Warren?*

He made it there unobstructed. He opened the door and walked into a room only he could make sense out of. He cleared some papers from his keyboard and hesitated before he tapped a key. It cleared the screen saver and brought up a profile document of Jill Bushing. He looked at it before sitting down. He scratched his eyebrow then threw himself into his chair. He continued to look at the picture. After a second, he sighed and leaned back with clinched fingers supporting the back of his head. *Shit, that damn Mason Bushing feeling again. But at least she's a lot better looking than that gnarly husband of hers. At least the way he looks now.*

He fished through some of the papers and held up another profile document. This one was of Mason. "The first thing we do in a case like this is find some truth," he said out loud to himself. He held up the picture of Mason to the screen. "I know where I can find Mason; there ain't no truth there, so where would this sweet thing be hiding?" He brought up a print window on the monitor, pressed enter, and got up.

Warren left his office, entered the hallway, and made his way toward another room down the hall. Suddenly, he heard a loud voice echo. He cringed.

"Just tell me how much already."

For a split second, he thought he was caught by a curious well-wisher, but it was obvious this was a problem for someone else. Warren sighed, realizing he was free again. He ignored it and continued to the print room.

"From what I just saw, if Mason stays here any longer,

he's gonna have to go back to that friggin' doctor he's been talking about."

Warren stopped dead in his tracks. He turned. At the end of the hallway, a large man and a slender woman stood at the booking desk.

Warren bolted back into his office. He grabbed his keyboard and hammered in some codes. Sure enough, the monitor showed Mason's bail and release documents. He snapped up his cell phone and touched the screen. He paced, waiting for a connection. He looked at the phone and continued pacing. "Fuckin' bureaucracy. No wonder I act like a damn Neanderthal," he muttered.

***

Warren stood behind the station doors. He watched the big guy lead the way and the woman help Mason make it through the courtyard. Warren spun around to look at the booking desk. His eyes fumed, but no one watched him. He clenched his fist slowly; his lips tightened. He turned back to the door. He was ready to unleash a beating on the door's window, but he stopped and calmed himself.

Mason looked back as he stumbled onto the sidewalk. Warren locked eyes with him then Mason turned the corner and walked out of sight.

CHAPTER 16

Warren drove in his unmarked police car that wasn't much different than his office: scattered papers, empty coffee cups. It was basically a moving dump that desperately needed some auto detailing, but it was his. No one else drove it. No one else cleaned it. No one else even went in it. He felt comfort knowing there was never a threat of being distracted with annoying queries about his wellbeing. This was the way it would have to be for Warren. He needed to be alone and busy for him to move on. After all, it was his wellbeing that brought him back to work; and when Warren worked, he worked cases, alone.

He thought that even though this case had a bizarre, almost sick feeling for him, it would be good therapy. Another criminal to look into might not have hit so close to home, but Rocksbrough didn't have a pile he could pick and choose from. All he needed to do was stay focused on the process, and this case needed the leg work done just like any other.

He stopped at the light in front of the grocery store in downtown Rocksbrough. He thought about this being a nice, small town. It was no wonder he met Linda here. But a crazy fucker like Mason Bushing? How could a quiet place like this spit out a guy who expects everyone to believe his insane accusations? Probably its naivety drew him here in the first place. Sayin' this type of shit in a big city... There was no chance he would even think of that. Warren nodded as the light turned green. He slowly drove along the main street thinking Mason must have scouted this place out. He made a mental note to look up how long he had been here.

After a few blocks, he was out of the downtown section and slowing down for a corner. *And what better place for him to settle into.* The dumping ground of Rocksbrough. It was dismal out here. Absent of anyone doing yard work, or any kids playing. In Warren's mind, this is where all the liars, cheaters, manipulators, and con artists came up with their scheming plans. But as far as he could tell, Mason's masquerade beat them all. *He must be the talk of the gutter around here.*

He drove with the random, but consistent, crackle from headquarters' dispatch as he turned onto Maple Avenue. He moved slowly, checking numbers on the houses that had one.

He stopped in front of Reg and Stace's house. A printout on the passenger seat confirmed the correct address. He crept forward a bit for a closer look at Mason's place next door then glanced at another document for confirmation. He studied both properties then scanned the surrounding area. With a slow nod and one more glance at the houses, he took his cell phone from the dash and snapped a quick picture of both.

He pulled away.

***

Still being entertained only by his dispatcher's broken up voice, Warren turned into Rocksbrough Heights. He drove along the entry road while checking another document. He turned and slowly moved along another street. All the things missing on Maple Avenue were here in abundance. *Death of a loved one looks good on ya, Jill Bushing.* The printout confirmed the address where he stopped, snapped another picture, and left.

***

Warren walked through the main doors and past the welcome sign for Rocksbrough Memorial Hospital. This was hardly the first time he'd been here, so he knew exactly where to go. He took a second to verify the elevator he needed then promptly stepped toward it so he wouldn't miss the opened door.

***

While exiting the elevator, Warren instinctively pulled out his police badge then checked which way the nursing station was. He proceeded there and showed a nurse his badge. He smiled and said, "Tom Simpson please." She looked him up and down. She took a long look at his badge then directed him to a room down the hall.

*****

Warren walked into room 515. Tom lay in the bed, asleep or dead, it was hard to tell. The working monitoring equipment and another nurse changing his intravenous confirmed Tom was still with them.

The nurse looked up. "Sorry, but he can't have any visitors."

Warren flashed his badge. "I'm a detective. I need to ask him some questions."

The nurse chuckled. "I don't think so. He's not quite with it right now." She continued to work.

"Has he been out for long?"

"The better question would be, has he been in at all?" She smiled which wasn't very useful.

"Ummm. Guess I'll pull up a chair and watch his monitor for you."

"Is that what happens to my extremely low nurse wages? Maybe you should go crackdown on hallway wheelchair offenders."

Warren laughed it off. Most people showed respect, or fear, or something that put him in the driver's seat when he showed his badge; but there were always the ones who felt the challenge. He noticed her name tag pinned to her uniform. "I'm not sure this is what I came here for, Karen." He smiled.

The door swung wide open. Warren watched a hot chick, with a major bitch on, march into the room. She carried a duffle bag too full to close.

She looked at him, then Karen. "Isn't the rule no visitors? Why is that so hard to understand?" She turned to Warren. "Who the fuck are you?"

"Now this is more like it," Warren said to Karen with bold anticipation.

"Show her the badge. She'll be impressed," Karen countered.

"You must be Mason's wife. I'm a cop. Detective—"

She dropped the bag. "Mason's wife? I was Mason's wife, when he was alive. Now I'm just Jill."

"We have a guy downtown who claims you're his wife." Warren watched Karen finish with the intravenous, pack up her equipment, and leave.

"The guy you have downtown almost killed my boyfriend. Do your job and find out who he is," Jill said as though she was in total command. She started going through the bag.

"That's why I'm here, Jill. You see, with insurance fraud—" He stopped to be sure he had her attention. "There's always an innocent victim, or two."

She stopped, looked up. "Who's the bad guy here?"

"You're leading the way, Jill. Poor Tom here is a nice touch, but the bag? Looks like you're sending him packin'. It's nice of you to do the heavy lifting for him though." Warren waited for a response but got none. "And then there's this." He pulled out his cell phone and brought up the picture of the house on Maple Avenue. He showed it to her.

Reluctantly, she looked then immediately turned away.

Quickly, Warren brought up the picture of her house in Rocksbrough Heights. "I can see buying a car, but why a new house?" He put his phone away when he saw she didn't need to see the picture. He leaned up against the wall.

Jill went back to the bag.

"I'll tell you what I think."

"Must you?" Jill said without looking up.

"Yea, I think I should," Warren said. "On the surface, it looks like you wanted to start fresh after poor Mason passed. A new guy…" He motioned to Tom. "Although he's looking a little used up right now." He gave Jill a shrug. "A new car— makes sense—and a fucking fantastic huge new house." He opened his arms up, begging for a response. "Shit, Jill, did you leave anything for groceries?"

He moved from the wall for a new vantage point. "If you didn't buy the house I wouldn't be all that concerned, but since you did I have to ask why. It could be that you planned this with Mason so when he came back with a new identity, you would be like, a totally new couple. But obviously you would do that in a completely new place. Somewhere like where you're planning to ship poor old Tom here." He stopped for a thinking break and the hope of some reaction.

Jill stopped going through the bag. She looked straight at him as if she was going to jump into the conversation, but Warren wasn't finished.

"Or, you decided Mason was too much baggage. The new house would look like you're his healed widow. When he comes back, you scream fraud which is right where we are now. Either way, if this Mason turns out to be your Mason, where does that leave you?" Warren stopped. *Your turn.*

She stood straight up to him. "Look, my boyfriend almost died in a fight with a guy who claims to be my dead husband. Did you hear that, *my dead husband?* You keep going on like he's alive. Mason Bushing is dead. And since he's dead, I bought a house. Big fuckin' deal."

"Hey, if this guy is playin' you for the insurance take, then carry on, Jill Bushing. We'll deal with our version of Mason Bushing, and you can live happily with whatever's left of Tom." He looked at Tom who was still out of touch with the real world. "But really, Jill, it's not as simple as that. Your problem with that theory is I don't think Mason's dead, so I have to figure out why you bought the *fucking fantastic huge new* house." He pressed her with his eyes to make sure that point sunk in. "Maybe the scam is all on Mason; you have nothing to do with it. If that's the case then again, carry on, Jill."

She took a step toward the door but stopped. "Okay, what if he is Mason? What happens to everything I've got then?"

Warren noticed that any confidence she showed suddenly

disappeared with that statement. She started for the door again. "Holy shit. We're talkin' about your dearly departed here." Warren stepped in her way and pushed the door closed a bit. "If that's the case then celebrate. He's alive. But don't blow up too many balloons because the insurance company taking back your riches won't be your biggest problem. The fraud charges I come down with will outweigh your heavy loss in social status, and believe me Jill Bushing, your name is going on those papers." He stepped aside to let her pass. He watched her continue to the door saying nothing, but the look on her face said she knew she was fucked.

"Of course there's always the chance Mason is telling the truth in one way or another. What do you think, Jill? Is there any chance of that?" Warren said.

Jill continued walking.

"Naw, me either; but it never hurts to ask, right?" He watched her pull the door open. "Hey, before you go I have to ask. Where did you dig Mason's hole?"

Jill stopped in the doorway but didn't look back. She took a deep breath and left.

CHAPTER 17

Another nurse, Candice, approached the busy hub of the hospital's fifth floor. It was the nursing station where Karen worked at the supply counter, loading up her cart. Candice joined her. "Hey, Karen, you naughty little bitch. I saw you come from 515," she said with a smile and conniving eyes.

Karen smirked.

Candice began to unload her cart then she nudged Karen. She looked back to the door of room 515. "You shoulda taken him with you, don't you think?"

"He's a cop; a detective. He'll probably be quick to point that out," Karen said as though there was no doubt about Candice's next move.

Candice worked fast to finish unloading then took off down the hall, pushing her empty cart. She got to the elevator as the doors closed. "Augh, damn," she said louder than necessary.

The doors opened. Candice entered quickly with her cart. She intentionally scanned the control panel and noticed the only button lit—L (lobby). "Going down?" she said to the elevator's only occupant.

"Certainly. What floor?"

"Three, then I'm gone. You too, right?" Candice stood there but there was no response from the occupant. "Shame isn't it?" The doors opened. Candice began to leave. "Augh, I wanted to hear you say detective," she said a little slutty like.

Suddenly, Candice became serious. She continued down the hall without looking back. She walked, with her cart, to the floor's nursing station. A quick look confirmed it was unoccupied. Her timing was perfect.

She stopped at the supply desk and began loading her cart with pills according to a patient sheet she had clipped to a chart board. With a quick hand, she slipped a syringe into her pocket. She pushed the cart aside and left the nursing station.

Candice continued down the hall and went into a family washroom. Inside, she quickly locked the door and took out the syringe and a vial full of black liquid with a hand printed label, *Purify 14 - Serum.* She filled the syringe, capped it, and pocketed both.

***

Candice walked into a private room where a patient slept. She stopped her cart beside the bed and took his hand. He slowly opened his eyes. She smiled and stroked his hand. "How are things today, Dave?" she said sympathetically.

His expression didn't change. Dave's eyes said it all—the end was near.

Candice took her patient chart and checked the medication documented under Dave's name. She swung the bed tray in front of him then put his meds there.

Dave struggled with the simple task of taking the pills while Candice prepared water. As he slowly drank, she checked his monitoring equipment then his intravenous drip. She looked toward the door.

She slipped the syringe from her pocket, flipped off the cap which fell back into her pocket and quickly injected him under the intravenous needle.

Dave was shocked, but he was too weak to put up much of a fight. He spilt the water; he tried to stop her, but the black fluid was gone before he could do anything.

Candice pocketed the syringe and began to stroke Dave's arm. She looked into his pleading eyes and offered him comfort with hers. "You're a lucky man, Dave." She watched his eyes roll back. "Soon, you'll be purified." Candice knew the concept well, and to her it sounded perfect.

Dave faded quickly. Calmly, Candice recapped the syringe in her pocket and cleaned up around the bed while Dave's fight ended. She looked at the monitor. It started to react then it flatlined.

Candice rushed out of the room. "Code blue. Code blue in 325B."

CHAPTER 18

With an ambulance siren screaming nearby, Dr. Nichols exited the elevator that joined the hospital to its parking garage. By the time he made his way through a set of doors and into the dreary garage, the siren had stopped, so he walked alone in silence.

It had been a busy week for Dr. Nichols. He was required at the police department for things like Mason's examination. His office waiting room was constantly full because he spent too much time dealing with police matters. Now he was here to follow up on the poor bastards he couldn't do anything for from his office. Even though this garage was not his first choice for down time, its quietness provided him with some much needed solitude.

He started down a row but realized he had forgotten where he parked. He looked around to get his bearings straight. After a few seconds, he headed in another direction. During all the time he spent looking for his car, he walked alone with only the echo from his shuffling feet. For some reason, it sounded many times louder than seemed normal to him—like a heartbeat in a stethoscope. It wasn't like this place was any less popular than usual, just at this particular time, nothing moved. He passed it off with the twitch of his mouth and continued up the row after seeing what he was looking for.

He approached his car. A noise echoed which made him turn quickly, but he saw nothing. He continued to his car, searching for his keys in his practitioner's bag. At his car door, he looked up.

***

Andrew stood behind the car. "Excuse me. Nichols right?"

Dr. Nichols looked up. "Doctor Nichols—yes. Do I know you?"

Andrew lunged at him with a knife extended. It penetrated his abdomen before Dr. Nichols could protect himself, even though he tried with the bag. Dr. Nichols appeared stunned. He had no defensive reaction at all. He lowered the bag and looked. Andrew just watched Dr. Nichols's eyes grow as fast as the small blood spot on his white shirt. He looked up at Andrew who was positioned for another blow. Dr. Nichols raised the bag instinctively, but that was short lived as his arms quickly lost strength. The bag fell to the ground. Andrew did nothing as Dr. Nichols's body went limp. Dr. Nichols gasped for air and collapsed onto the side of his car. He desperately tried to breathe which quickly resulted in blood bubbling from his mouth.

Andrew surged again. This time he caught Dr. Nichols and held his head from behind with his hand covering his mouth. He wrapped the other arm around his abdomen and drove the knife into his chest again. He held the knife there; he twisted it a bit, then Andrew held him like he actually cared. He guided Dr. Nichols softly to the ground while driving the knife in further one last time.

Andrew let Dr. Nichols's lifeless body slide out of his arms. He calmly wiped his hand on Dr. Nichols's jacket and got up checking for any blood that may have gotten on him. There was none except some remaining on his hand. He pulled on Dr. Nichols's shirt then wiped it and the knife. Then he walked away unnoticed.

CHAPTER 19

Mason sat on the toilet in a bathroom that could barely accommodate it, the sink, and a tub; all of which desperately needed replacement. He looked around the room which felt like luxury compared to the cell in the basement of the police department or Dr. Harlow's laboratory prison. It had nothing to do with the size of the room or the condition of its accommodations. It was all about freedom. Here it was like wide open fields compared to the confined outhouses he'd been in before.

He couldn't believe that in a few short days he had come full circle—from Stace and Reg's house, to being a prisoner again, and back here with nothing to show for it except a body full of bruises. The escape from Dr. Harlow was supposed to be a clean break, but somehow things had taken a horrible turn. *Clean break… How the hell could I possibly think this would go down any better than it did?* Being back here gave him another chance though. Since Mason was no stranger to adversity, he should be able to dust himself off and go at it again, given enough time to recover. It was that recovery part, both physically and mentally, that concerned him. It seemed like every time he had this chance, he was knocked back down again. Now he wondered if his body would just give up.

Although the police brutality had taken its toll, it was nothing compared to what he had already endured. He wiggled his toes, amazed they still actually worked. He pressed them into the floor. The white and red stress marks were proof the body those feet carried fully functioned and could continue on. This was very different from the way he felt before the escape, before the capture, before everything changed.

Cancer had been a real shocker for Mason. Before that, he would have been a prime candidate as a men's underwear model. Chiseled to perfection, he was amazed himself the disease had picked him to mess with. But it turned out his body was no match for the malignant cells that had taken over. Even though the doctors reassured him chemo and radiation were the answer, they did very little except take him down even further.

After that, it became obvious Mason was doomed. His prognosis was death, to the point of a countdown, but the pain that settled in became his immediate cause for concern. This had been real pain—as much as any body could endure.

The pain he tried to get over now paled in comparison, and it had been only drugs that could bring that cancer agony to a tolerable threshold. But of course, drugs only masked the problem, and those rapidly growing cells continued to wreak havoc on the body Mason had worked so hard to create.

Mason rubbed his hands hard along his thighs. It was relieving to feel living flesh he had thought was gone long ago. Just as he had come full circle in the past few days, he was also in that process on a much larger scale—life to death to life again.

This body was not as it had been though. On the surface it was the same skin; the same hair; the same nails, and moles, and birthmarks. But inside it felt much different. Even though Mason had been in excellent shape, he always felt used up from the hard work of getting it to look better than it actually was. Now, he felt new. Not fit or rock solid but new. The process Dr. Harlow had taken him through broke him down for sure, even lower than where cancer had taken him, if that was even possible. But it also built him back up. Mason didn't know what ran through his veins now, but whatever it was, it beat the shit out of cancer and this new ride would hopefully make up for lost time.

He took some toilet paper to finish his business. He wiped once—a clean sheet. *Awesome. Even that's working to perfection.* He got up and stood naked in front of the mirror. He felt a sense of relief that he could finally see his full reflection. It was a basic human privilege that was taken away during captivity with Dr. Harlow. Perhaps there were no mirrors to prevent those being held from seeing the effects of what he was doing, but it was probably just a simple way to keep the captive, and himself, alive. But Mason could see all of himself now, and what he looked at was a poor excuse for the freedom he searched for. From his legs down he was fine, but up here was a completely different story.

His eyes were fully opened and the swelling on his face was gone, but the gothic rainbow that remained was more than he could take. There had been a day, before any of this happened, when Mason could easily handle a guy who was angered because of a simple missing tooth. Since then, two years had passed and the body Mason looked at now showed the effects of what he had been through. Most of the deterioration came after chemo started, but Dr. Harlow's rebirth therapy definitely didn't help.

He looked at his bicep. He flexed it then his tricep. He used to have a broad chest that flowed seamlessly into flat, ripped abs. This had been framed with defined traps and strong lats to complete an upper body that others drooled over. Sure the muscle tone was still there, but the mass and chiseled definition was gone. Although he wasn't carrying much body fat, what he looked at left him feeling like the shower curtain behind him could smother him whole if he wasn't careful.

He turned his hip to see the bump Dr. Nichols discovered, and a sudden flood of concern took over his thoughts. The look on his face said it all—he'd been down this road before, but suddenly he realized the bump was gone. He touched the area, rubbed it, and shifted for a better look. There was nothing, like it was never there. He checked the other side to be sure he was looking in the right spot. There was nothing there either. He used the mirror—again, nothing. *Was it really possible cancer had come back, and Harlow's wonder drug had taken care of it already?* He looked at himself again in the mirror. *How could it be? And if it was true, why the hell would Harlow be doing all of this way out in the middle of nowhere with people who were supposed to be dead? What was it Dr. Nichols said? The crazy military scientist…turned down for grants over and over…so he went underground. Harlow wasn't capable of all of this. The fuckin' creep was, crazy.* Mason stared deeply into his own eyes. *Why, Mason, after all I've done for you,* he remembered Dr. Harlow saying again. *What the hell am I? What has this, genius, done?* He shook his head to clear these thoughts but it didn't help. He stepped back to get a fuller prospective.

Well, with the good, comes the bad I guess. If there was any bad… So far, physically, he was fine. Skinny for sure, but other than that, fine. But Mason was having trouble accepting the thought that his problems were over. There simply had to be a price to pay. Maybe the price was inevitably coming with that detective guy, Warren. Physically though, he was problem free. Whatever the case, Mason knew there was no way a guy like him would be blessed with life after death and not somehow have to justify it. He'd never won a lottery before, and there was little chance his luck had suddenly changed.

He tried to think of what to expect, but he came up blank.

Are you the right man for the job, whatever that might be? His reflection stared back, but no expression on his face provided the answer. He figured he was going to have to wait to find out, and he had more pressing matters to deal with right now anyway.

He took one last look at himself before he stepped into the shower, cautiously pulling the curtain closed.

CHAPTER 20

Stace thought that the basement of a one hundred and fifty year old house was hardly the place to spend the afternoon, but if laundry had to be done, this is where she did it. Most people who lived on the street gathered up all their dirty stuff and hauled it to the Clean Sudz Laundromat at the strip mall two blocks away. At least she had her own machines, so she considered herself lucky. She couldn't spend much time here anyway. She had two young kids upstairs, so whatever she did in the basement was done quickly.

While she sorted clothes for her next load, the dryer stopped which left the sound of water, rushing down the cast iron main drain, the only noise in this dreary place. She stopped sorting and looked at the pipe. Of course she knew it was Mason up there, not more than ten feet away. This was the same man who she, Reg, and Jill had buried a year ago.

That disastrous change in her life was somehow being wound back for a chance to start all over. It looked like this time though, it would be without Jill which was no loss for Stace. Jill had never been much a part of what she and Reg had with Mason. She had been there physically, but Stace never really liked her. Stace felt like she could see right through her.

Stace knew Jill's type—hidden agendas, two-faced conversations—girl talk really that she wanted no part of. She hadn't been much different than any other girl Stace had crossed paths with during her life, so she could kind of understand Mason's infatuation with her. Who else would he have chosen? She was hot, there was no doubt about that, and she was very different with men than she was with women. One of the problems Stace had with her had been exactly that—the way she acted around men. She flirted, admired, and encouraged them almost to the point of being slutty. *No, she was slutty.* Not just with Mason, but all men, Reg included. Stace had brought this up with Mason a few times, but he just brushed it off. She never really harped on it because it hadn't been her problem anyway. She had enough of her own.

One of those problems had been the cancer Mason got. To Jill, Mason's cancer simply got in her way. Stace could see that Jill's master plan had been suddenly flawed, and Jill was preoccupied figuring out what to do next. That left Stace with the task of tending to Mason. She didn't mind really. If Mason was going to die, it was her way of spending the most time with him that she could. But watching Jill going through the motions and really just waiting it out, bothered Stace to the point where there was simply no relationship between them. So when Mason died, Jill might as well have died too.

Stace started pulling clothes from the dryer, but continued thinking about how Mason had always been different for her. He was no doubt Reg's best friend, but he was also the only friend Stace ever had. Mason was the person she would confide in when she had problems, mostly in her relationship with Reg; and Mason always came to Stace with his, which undoubtedly seemed to be about Jill. They talked about the reality shows Stace liked, Reg's mother who had Alzheimer's disease, what to buy the kids for their birthdays, why Stace couldn't sleep anymore. They even planned what she should make for dinner considering Reg's huge appetite.

It didn't bother Stace much that she had no girlfriends to do things like that with. Mason was a good listener. What difference did it make if they weren't the same sex? Anyone she had gotten close to, from grade school, through high school, and into adulthood, never gave her the feeling of trust Mason did. Whenever she got close to another girl, she always ended up being stabbed in the back. Others were able to let things like that go, but not Stace. She didn't hold grudges, but she didn't stick around either. She always felt she was much better off with guys anyway.

Reg was the first person she ever had a lasting relationship with. In the beginning, it was easy. He was funny, caring. He was a protector, but he was never the deep, emotional type. They got married without being together long, and it had been good. Then, Mason showed up.

Should she have waited it out? Should she had done something before it was too late? Should she take what hadn't been hers and violate everything she believed in? These were questions Stace would ask herself but refused to answer. Mason gave her everything she had been missing, and she was happy for that. Maybe that was enough she always thought. But then Mason died, and all that trust went away. She still trusted Reg; she always had, but there was something about the deeper trust she had with Mason that came from her ability to tell him anything. So now Stace found herself spending more time alone, doing things like laundry in the basement.

While she emptied wet clothes from the washer and threw them into the dryer, she couldn't help but wonder how things with Mason would be different from here on. It was great that he was back in her life, but he was obviously involved in something deep. Even though Stace wanted to give Mason his space, she and Reg were involved now, especially since he was living with them. *How is that going to affect me? What about Kyle and Emma?* Mason was great with the kids, but this was a new Mason. This Mason had problems unlike anything he'd had before. She stopped working for a second then started loading her half sorted pile into the washer while her thoughts about Mason continued.

Even with what he was going through right now, he was still the same Mason, and she was still the same Stace. If anyone could get deep into his head, it would be her. Up until this point, she hadn't had a chance to do any of that; but she needed to, and she knew it. It was just a matter of when and where. When it happened, this uneasiness she felt would be gone, hopefully.

She wanted to believe him up front, but Reg's insurance theory made a whole lot more sense than the crazy doctor story. Even if Mason wasn't willing to admit he was lying, Stace was pretty sure he would admit it to her. At least the old Mason would have. And with that admission, Stace was confident that Mason knew it would go no further. But maybe Stace wouldn't be able to crack the seal of this Mason, or maybe there was no lie to overcome. The new Mason had a lot to deal with, so maybe he had already made the decision to ride this one out on his own.

However it turned out, Stace worried about him and she needed to know how he was going to handle it. How would he deal with the charges being laid against him? She threw in the last sorted piece of clothes. How would he deal with starting all over? She started throwing in stuff from the unsorted pile, selecting the right pieces, one at a time. How would he get money? She started throwing in any piece. How would he pay back Reg and her for the bail? She stopped with the clothes. *What if this guy upstairs, in my damn shower, isn't Mason at all?* The water rushing through the pipes seemed to suddenly run faster like the blood rushing through her veins. *Jesus Christ. Stop. Just Stop.* She closed her eyes and sighed. She looked back to the main drain; the ceiling. She started the washer, then the dryer. *There, that should be enough noise to drown out this craziness for good.*

Suddenly, she realized, the kids. *Shit.* She turned quick and leaped over the laundry baskets. She bolted for the stairs.

CHAPTER 21

S tace was done in the basement and now worked at the much preferred kitchen sink. The stove would be even more of a treat because she would rather be creating than cleaning up. The window above the kitchen sink made this a better alternative than the dismal laundry tub though, so she was somewhat pleased. And of course, the kids were in the next room. Whether or not that was a good thing, it was much more relaxing knowing trouble was no farther than an arm's reach away.

So she worked reasonably happy until Emma started to cry. This was a common occurrence sure, but with recent activities and now this piled on top, patience around here was at an all-time breaking point. At first Stace ignored it, but it wasn't long before noise from the quickly evolving fight rose above what was playing on the television. *I wonder if I look surprised. The only shocking thing here is that I actually got a load done.*

"Aaah, Mommy. Kyle's taking my bear," Emma complained.

Stace kept her cool. "Kyle, leave Emma's things alone." She started to rinse out a dishcloth.

Emma continued crying, and the fight got louder. Kyle's refusal to cooperate came with his claim for the toy in question. "It's not yours. It's mine."

Stace stopped what she was doing. She squeezed hard on the dishcloth and dropped it in the sink. She sighed and looked out the window hoping to see something that would help her get away from this. All she saw was a blue van that drove by slowly which meant nothing to her, just like what she got from looking out the window in the first place.

Emma came running into the kitchen with her eyes overflowing. "Mommy, Mommy. He won't give Teddy back."

Stace turned around quickly. She yelled, "*Kyle, that bear is not yours!*" She rushed past Emma into the hallway leading to the living room.

Kyle stood in the middle of the room with a bear in his hand. She saw that guilt was his only excuse. "How many times, Kyle? How many times do you have to be told? *That is not your bear.*" Stace took it away aggressively. "You have plenty of your own toys, don't you?" Her eyes bared down on him meaning nothing but business.

Kyle looked away. He tried to leave.

She grabbed him by the chin to keep his focus on her.

"Kyle—" She let go, suddenly concerned about her aggressiveness. "I'm going to tell you one more time, Kyle." She showed him the bear. "You let Emma play with her toys." She stared him down. "Okay?"

Kyle nodded. He looked embarrassed by the scolding.

"Okay." She went to get the remote lying on an end table. "You just watch some TV while I put Emma down for a nap."

Emma ran off behind the sofa. "Nooo. I don't wanna sleep."

"Emma, get back here." Stace took the remote and flipped randomly through channels. She looked back to Kyle. "Come here, Kyle."

Kyle slowly walked toward her.

Stace gave him the remote. "Find a show and be good," she said then hurried to the sofa and grabbed Emma. "Come here you little screamer."

Stace held Emma in one arm and left the living room heading to the hallway. After a few steps, she pushed the bathroom door open.

Mason turned quickly. He was fully naked.

"Holy shit." Stace stepped back and leaned against the wall. She started to laugh. "Sorry, Mason. I forgot you were—"

The door slammed shut.

"I bet."

Chaotic noise radiated from the bathroom.

"What the hell are you laughing at anyway?" Mason said

followed by a bang and a groan.

Stace didn't move, but she couldn't stop laughing. She looked at Emma in her arms who didn't have a clue what just happened. "No, Mason, seriously. I'm sorry."

"Yeah, you sound serious."

"Are you okay? That groan sounded like you're desperate to finish something."

Mason stepped out of the bathroom covered with a towel. She watched him walk by smiling.

"In a hurry?" He walked into his room—Kyle's room actually. "Hi, Emma."

Stace stood there holding Emma and smiling huge. Mason looked back with a wink. Stace continued smiling and pulled Emma in close to her, blocking her eyes.

CHAPTER 22

Mason wore shorts when he walked toward the kitchen—only shorts. He knew Stace was there, and by the sounds of it, she was alone. He stopped at the entrance, reluctant to get in her way when she was, creating.

"Who turned off the lights in Kiddyland?" Mason said then leaned against the wall after deciding he went far enough. From this distance, he liked watching her work. Her movements, her flow, her graceful actions always made a hectic environment seem calm.

He watched Stace stir her creation in an eight quart soup pot on the stove.

"I put Emma to bed. Kyle's watching TV." She turned to him. She looked away and began to laugh. "I was just thinking."

"About what?"

"Oh, something I saw."

Mason stepped forward and leaned up against the counter. He stared at her. "Recently?"

"Yeah, kinda."

Mason continued staring making Stace uncomfortable. He realized that watching her close up was just as good as watching from a distance. It was better actually. It had been so long since he'd seen her alone or felt anything remotely like this. But her smile disappeared. Now she looked worried.

"Can you feel your face yet? You look better."

Mason nodded. "Can't complain I guess considering where I should be. Actually, you know, I can complain; and I should complain. Those bastards beat the royal shit out of me, and what did I do? I walked away; said nothing, and now I'm waiting for them to slam me again with charges."

"You did the right thing, Mason. None of those assault charges will stick."

"Assault charges... What about fraud?" Stace's eyes avoided his. He watched her look at the bruising on his face, then lower.

"You look good, Mason."

Mason shrugged. "If you like bones in your soup." He knew she was checking him out, and he did nothing to stop her. It felt good having someone close to him on his side. He enjoyed having her enjoying him.

Stace turned back to the soup pot. "Trust me, you look good." She paused, lost for words. "And there ain't no bones in this soup."

Mason said, "Cream of Carrot?"

She smiled and nodded.

"Carrots, sweet and regular potatoes, chicken broth." He stopped for confirmation.

Stace nodded again but stayed focused on the soup.

"Garlic, onions, salt, pepper and thyme," he said with raised eyebrows, a nod, and a head tilt.

Stace laughed softly. She shook her head. "That pretty much confirms it," she said quietly, almost to herself.

"Confirms what?" he asked, already knowing the answer. "I am who I say I am, Skillet. Nothing I've told you guys is a lie. I know it must be hard to believe, but Christ, Skillet, I need someone on my side."

"I do believe you, Mason," she said, turning to face him.

"But you don't want me here, do you?"

"Of course I want you here." She paused seeming unsure how to continue. "It just brings back memories I don't want to remember."

"Skillet, what happened between us never should have. It just did."

"Yes, it did, and after that, I couldn't have you. Then I lost you for good." She turned away, as if she was ashamed. "There were times when I thought it was better that way, and I hated myself for it. There were also times when I hoped you were watching me." She looked him in the eyes again. "I've made love to myself hoping you were watching, Mason."

Stace walked to the hallway. He watched her check on Kyle.

She turned back to him. "I love Reg. I really do. I don't want to hurt him."

"I didn't come here to dig up dirt. I came for my life, not yours," he said and he meant it, but it was the hardest thing for him to have to live by.

She walked forward looking straight at him. Focused, passionate, sexual. "I know, Mason. But you're here, and…" She stopped before getting too close. The soup started to boil over. "Shit." She ran to it.

Mason sighed and stepped away from the counter. "I'll leave soon. When I get things straight with Jill." He sat down at the table making sure he looked at anything but Stace. He knew she was working on the soup. From the corner of his eye, he noticed her shaking her head.

"You can stay as long as you want, or at least until I can't take anymore."

He looked back to her as she got the soup under control. She turned to him, looking only at his face this time.

"Does it hurt?" She stepped toward him and reached out to touch his bad eye.

"Not as much as it should. Reg, he's my best friend." Mason saw the soft look she gave him.

She gently touched his eye. She cupped his cheek in her hand. "Shit, Mason. What are you gonna do?" She smiled cautiously. She turned away and went to the stove then began clearing a dirty pot and a frying pan.

Mason stared face down at the table. "I'm not sure what I can do."

"What about Jill? If you can get her to believe—"

"She knows it's me, she just doesn't care. I don't get how she can be like that. I die then I'm alive, and she prefers me dead."

"She's like that because that's exactly Jill," she said while she started rinsing the frying pan.

Mason looked back to Stace. "Not the Jill I know, or knew. The Jill I married. The Jill I loved."

"Mason, she was never any different. You just refused to see it." Stace stopped the water. She leaned back against the counter. "Jill has always been about clinging to someone who would get it all done for her. Then you died and left her a money tree. Man, in Jill's eyes, that was even better than cashin' in on the lottery because she didn't have to go out and buy a ticket."

Mason continued watching her. She stopped talking and turned back to the sink and the dishes.

"Of course, if you were alive, you would have bought the ticket for her, right?"

At first Mason did nothing and said nothing, then he started nodding slowly. This was hard to swallow, even coming from the person who knew it best.

A knock from the front door, jolted Mason back to reality. He could see right away who it was, but he didn't move. He just gripped his hand tight, into a fist, and sat hoping to wait it out. He watched Stace go to the door, and Warren standing on the porch.

"Hello, Ma'am. I'm looking for Mason Bushing. I'm

Detective Warren Fillmore."

Stace turned to Mason. "Did you hear that?"

He nodded but stayed sitting. *Well, I made it through a couple nights and almost two full days. Guess I should feel lucky.*

Warren looked through the screen door, past Stace and straight at Mason. "Got a minute?"

Mason said, "Is that how long it takes to charge me again?"

"No, no, shit, man. I've barely got my feet wet with this one. I just have some questions, and some, what do I call them, developments."

"The last time I talked to you I ended up looking like this. I don't think I'm interested in doubling down, at least not until I recover some of my lost pride."

"Hey, man, none of that came from my work," Warren said then squinched up his face a bit. "Maybe a little in the basement, but, Mason, you must be lucky today. I'm working on channeling my inner aggression." He smiled at Stace. "Is that how you say that kinda thing?"

Mason looked for her reaction, but the expression on her face made it clear she didn't find it funny. He looked back to Warren who raised his eyes with a half-smile.

"Seriously, man, we have to talk. This isn't going to go away any time soon. Actually, it's a lot like you. It's gonna keep coming back," he said with another cocky smile.

Mason didn't laugh either.

"Christ, tough audience. I'm tryin' to go easy here, Mason."

Mason lightened up a bit. *Might as well hear what he has to say. What choice do I have really?* "All right then, fire," he said somewhat reluctantly.

"I'll only do that if you start to run." Warren smiled then laughed at himself. "I'm in a good mood today, man. You should take advantage." He paused with a slight head shake. "Come on. Let's go for a walk."

"I prefer having the door on my side."

"Mason—" Warren looked in another direction—into the living room. He squinted. "He hasn't taken his eyes off me since I started talking, and he's not laughing at my jokes either."

Stace took off to the living room.

Mason scratched his head. He got up slowly and walked to the door. Then he stopped. *If I go any further, he'll probably roll me down the stairs and finish me for good.*

Warren walked down the steps, but Mason didn't follow him. Warren stopped and turned back at the bottom. "I went to see your punchin' bag. Got the pleasure of meetin' your sparring partner too," Warren said. "He didn't have much to say—nothing actually—and she seemed pissed to see me, like I was getting in the way of something. Do you know anything about that?"

"She thinks I'm someone else." Mason paused not sure how, or if, he should continue. *Watch what you say. Before you know it, he'll have it all fucked up just like they've done to my face.* "I told ya before. Go dig me up. I won't be there."

Mason felt Stace come up from behind him. He noticed

131

Kyle in her arms, so he opened the door and stepped onto the porch.

Warren nodded but it was obvious to Mason he was thinking—holding something back.

"She certainly wants you out of the picture. She's got a fortune to worry about."

Mason was steamed and it showed. *Fucker. Hit me where it hurts right off the bat.* "And how was I supposed to react to that?"

"Channel your inner feelings. Fuck me, I'm so good at this I'm teaching it already."

Mason sat down on the top step.

"When do you think she turned on you?"

Mason shook his head in frustration. This was the same question he had asked himself over and over, just in a very different context. He decided to keep that quiet. *Just let him talk; see where he's going.*

"Ummm. Dead air."

I bet you get that a lot. Though he really wished Warren wasn't there, he began to think that this may be of some value for him. At least Warren might know something he didn't.

"Just like Jill. Not much of a talker are ya? You guys actually do have something in common," Warren said with a reassuring nod. "Okay, I'll talk. How about I start at the beginning; the end for you," Warren said. "You keep telling me to dig you up, but why would I do that, Mason? Dental would easily solve that problem if I was the slightest bit concerned about who you actually are. But since I'm a dot-n-cross kinda guy, I asked her about it anyway." Warren paused with a reflective look. He looked away. "Did you love your wife, Mason?"

Mason didn't answer. *What kind of a fuckin' question is that? But don't ask anything about his wife.*

Warren looked back to him. "She didn't love you, did she?"

Mason replied cautiously, "Why?"

"She had you cremated."

"So?"

"And scattered." Mason knew Warren was watching for a reaction. "How does that screw things up? Or are the pieces perfectly in place?"

Again, Mason wasn't sure how to answer or if he should. *Say nothing. Just say nothing. But what do you mean she had me, or whatever, scattered?*

"Well, I'll tell you what I think."

You do that.

"At first I really wanted you two to be working together. I mean, that would have been great for you guys. Think about the romance. Struggling lovers looking for easy street. You show up somewhere else, and she's there with a whole whack of cash." He rolled his eyes. "But you ruined that story line by running back here with your arms waving high saying *I'm back, I'm back* and Jill—fuck, man, Jill bought a damn huge house." He twisted his head as if it desperately needed a crack.

Yeah, well, that's not even close. Got another pitch coming? I'm sure you do.

"So now I'm thinkin' you were in it together and she decided you carried too much weight. You caught on so you come running back with some fucked up story and—but wait, she bought a *God damn huge house*." He scratched his forehead and wrinkled his lips. "Are you starting to see my problem here, Mason?"

Your problem is you're so far down dreamer's lane, I have no idea how to get you back. Basics, man. Work with what you've got. "So you think we're Bonnie and Clyde?" Mason said.

"No, not anymore, and I don't think the scattered remains part has anything to do with any plan either. What do you think it means, Mason?"

Mason looked away feeling like a school boy in the Principal's office. At this point he just wanted to go back into the house, shut the door, and not hear what he knew Warren would say.

"I think she wanted you the fuck out of her life."

Bingo. You fuckin' moron.

"And that makes sense because now I've got you doin' this scam all by yourself."

Mason watched Warren stop with a thinking man's look.

"But when you came back, you quickly realized she— come on, Mason, all together now." Warren used his hands to orchestrate the session. "*Bought a fuckin' God damn huge house.* Then, Mason, get this. You show up at her door step— *Hi, honey, I'm back.* Fuck, man, that must have made her shit enough for ten."

Mason shook his head and let out a huge sigh. *So much for gaining some valuable information.* Mason turned away when Stace came back without Kyle. "How about just believing me?" Mason said with little confidence.

"Because that would be stupid. An insurance scam makes a whole lot more sense don't you think, Mason?"

Mason looked back to him, but he didn't answer.

"She got a million for ya. Did you know that?"

Mason shook his head but stayed quiet. *No, actually, I didn't. How much did you say?*

Warren started to walk to his car. "One more thing, Mason."

No, not one more thing. One Million. I signed an insurance policy for a million dollars?

"I didn't just come here to get you all fucked up, although I have to admit it was part of the plan." Warren looked back. "I actually have news for you too. Doctor Nichols, remember him? The guy who knew all about your little Purify alibi? Well, he was murdered in the hospital parking garage last night."

Mason knew Warren was looking at Stace now.

"Where were you last night, Mason?" He continued to stare Stace down. "Hope you're enjoying his company."

Mason sat shocked, not sure what to process first, or if he could deal with any of it at all. He looked back to see the confusion on Stace's face. Mason heard Warren's car door open.

"If you're not calling this your home, Mason, you should think about getting one. Drifters don't usually do well in court. Of course, I'm not sure how you're going to do that."

The engine started. Mason looked back to his car.

Warren started to back out of the driveway but stopped with his arm out the window. "Maybe Jill can help. She's got lots of room."

Mason watched him continue backing out with a smirk on his face.

CHAPTER 23

Mason sat in a designer, oversized sofa while he looked at the lavish French doors he just busted up to get in here. With an open can of beer, he turned to the widescreen. A ball game gave him some viewing pleasure, but Mason didn't pay attention. He was too busy checking out the room that was probably worth more than the whole house he had shared with Jill. The front window was right beside him providing a clear view of the road, driveway, and a new for sale sign on the front lawn.

He remembered Stace's unflattering words about Jill. At the time, she pretty much had him convinced of her self-centeredness. That really wasn't worth adding to the problems he already had. But if there was one thing consistent about Mason—one thing that drove him to make every decision he did—he had a mind of his own, and now that mind was on Jill. As much as he wanted to make things easier, this problem wasn't going away until he found out about his wife for himself.

Mason simply thought Jill now worked in look out for number one mode. When she found out she had more than anyone else, she tried to protect it. Who wouldn't? Now that she had it, she upped her social status. He always wanted to give her more, but what he gave her had been better than anyone else she knew. He figured she was fine. Looking around here made him realize he must have been wrong. If he really thought about it though, Jill was no different than anyone else—you work with what's in front of you. When someone drops a truckload on your lap, who's not going to overreact? *Shit. Even I would loosen up my belt a bit. Maybe not to this extent, but hey, what's done is done.* He sat back in the comfy couch with his fingers locked together, wrapped behind his head. He pretended to watch the game, but his mind was way too occupied for that.

Given some time, he thought he could get used to this. If this is what she really wanted, then what the hell. They might as well enjoy it because once all this identity and relationship stuff was straightened out, the insurance company would surely be knocking on that oversized door. He sat up and saw the for sale sign again from the corner of his eye. He focused on it. *First things first. That has got to go.*

He got up and walked around since a thorough inspection was definitely necessary if he was going to call this place home. Although it looked like money hadn't been part of the decision to buy it, Jill had done a real good job picking this beauty. Mason had no clue what she had paid for the place, but he knew what she got for him. She probably had laid down most of it on this. Of course, that didn't make a whole lot of sense which was just how Jill would think. She probably thought living in luxury sounded like a whole lot of fun, and she could just sell it when the novelty wore off. He was also quite sure she didn't expect that time to come so soon, which would be why she acted the way she did when she saw him.

Mason always thought he had a good thing going with Jill. Sure they fought, but it had never been about serious relationship issues. It usually had to do with his adventures with Reg, and more specifically, that those adventures hadn't included her. They met in a bar, and Jill was a bar girl at heart; but Reg never had taken Stace, so Mason would never take Jill. The fact that Stace never had a problem with it, left Mason envious of Reg, and armed with fuel for the next fight with Jill.

Maybe all the time they were together she had been fine, and she just wanted to be his center of attention. Maybe, it had been the insurance payout that changed her. That being the case, she would change again. He was sure of it. His sudden appearance may have been simply too much to process, and when she sees Mason here, right now, things would be different. At least that was his theory, and it justified a break and enter in the richest part of Rocksbrough.

Mason sat back down on the sofa. He took his beer and

shifted a little, straightening up for a closer look outside. While he was here, he had himself pretty much convinced he would get back with Jill but doubt still lingered. He took a drink and stared blankly at the window. Whatever the case, he was about to find out.

The Mustang pulled into the driveway, top down. Mason watched Jill get out, armed with shopping bags which made her look like a Vogue subscriber. She looked at the for sale sign as if this was the first time she'd seen it.

Mason positioned himself back into the couch making like he had always been here. *Just look like you own the place. Actually, I do kinda.* A smile stretched over his face, then the door opened.

When Jill entered, she immediately reacted to the television. "Damn, if it's going to turn itself on, at least it should find something worth watching," she said to herself.

Mason couldn't see her at first, but he didn't change his position. He didn't want her to freak out when she saw him. He just wanted to blend in.

He got his first glance of her when she walked into the kitchen. He had truly missed her. He wanted to take a second to enjoy her, unlike the other night when things got out of control. To Mason, she was magical to watch. He remembered everything that attracted him to her years ago, and he was warmed with those same feelings having not seen her for so long.

She moved beside the fridge and pulled out a chair to put her bags on. Mason popped his head up, but she didn't notice. "Grab me another beer will ya?" He held out his empty can, smiling like he couldn't be more comfortable.

Jill spun around shocked. Her bags hit the ground. She immediately went for a portable phone on the counter. She started punching out a number, then stopped. She looked at the phone.

"I had to cut the line to get in." Mason squinched up his face a bit. "Sorry." He got up. "You know, you can get systems that don't use the phone line."

She looked around frantically and saw the broken doors.

"Don't worry about those. I'll have 'em fixed up in no time," he said with the exact confidence he had been thinking about moments ago. He made his way through the living room and into the kitchen. He put the empty on the counter and stood directly in front of her. "So how much we gettin' for the house?" *Take over right away. That oughta swing her back my way.* "Probably best to wait it out and see what happens." He smiled at her. "Don't ya think?"

Jill looked shocked—trapped. She appeared to compose herself, but she failed. "Please don't hurt—"

"Woah, woah, Jill. Did you say hurt? No one's gettin' hurt, Jill." Mason went to the fridge and grabbed two beers with one hand. "Just good times from here on. My God, look at the place." He popped one open and offered it almost magician like. "Fun between you and me, like we've done a thousand times."

She started to move away. "You want money, right?" She ran for the stairway.

He realized quickly the casual approach wasn't going to work. He put both beers down. "The money's got nothing to do with what I want, Jill. I just want what we had. Is that really too much to ask?"

She turned before reaching the stairs. "It is when I have no idea who you are." She turned back and rushed away.

"Christ, Jill, drop the act. You know it's me." He bolted after her. He caught her before she got to the first step. He pulled her back by the shoulders but laid off right away.

Jill hunched over and held her arms tight in front of her. "Please don't. Just leave and I won't say anything about you ever being here," she whimpered.

"Just what the hell do you think I'm going to do? Shit, you act like I'm some fuckin' animal ready to unleash a brutal *whatever* on ya." He crouched down to see her buried face. The railing blocked him, like he was a prisoner behind balusters. "Jill, we've been together for as long as I can remember. We took the same thing in our coffee. You wore my boxers when we watched a movie. We drank the same beer; we brushed our teeth with the same toothbrush." He gently moved her arms away from her face. "We slept in the single bed together, Jill." He tried to get a glimpse of her eyes. "We did all the things two people in love do. How did me dying change that?"

She looked at him but started moving up the stairs. He did nothing to stop her. He expected her to turn around, and then everything would be fine. He was convinced. It was all too much, and she needed time to think it through. When she came around… Any second now, he knew she would come around.

Clear from Mason's reach, she did stop. She turned. "Mason's dead. You're telling me you're someone who doesn't exist." She rushed up the rest of the stairs. "Money, I'll give you more. Then go away."

That didn't sit well with Mason. How could she possibly look him in the eye and say he wasn't who she knew he was? How could she not want to start back where they left off? The only answer was money. Mason looked up the staircase. He looked at everything around him. She really was going for the money over him. Everything he thought about Jill suddenly changed. Stace had been right. He had been blinded all along. Jill was nothing but a gold digger even though there was no real gold until now.

Mason snapped. He chased her. "Is that all you want from me? To go away?" He got to the top of the stairs and saw her flee into a room down the hallway. He ran straight to the room.

When he entered, he stopped right away. It was the master bedroom and what he saw downstairs paled in comparison to what he looked at here—a bevel cut wall to wall mirror, a center chandelier, a canopy bed with matching draped window coverings and exquisite furniture.

Jill was frantically going through the drawer of a corner vanity set.

Mason rushed to her and spun her around. They were face to face. Bills fell from her hands. "Look at me. Look in my eyes. Listen to my voice." He forced her to stare at him. "Now, tell me I'm not your husband. Tell me you don't need our life back. Tell me you don't want me."

Jill was helpless. Tears filled her eyes. "My husband died over a year ago. Mason's dead." She paused with a stare that looked like she died herself. "Who wants a dead man?"

Mason loosened his grip on her, devastated by her words.

She slipped away. "Take the money. Just leave me alone." She rushed out the door.

Feet pounded on the stairs. Mason didn't move. He stared at the doorway—stunned and motionless. A door slammed shut. Mason took another look around the room when he heard a car engine start. Then there was silence.

Mason stood alone with money scattered at his feet.

CHAPTER 24

Stace drank a coffee while sitting on the porch with a purse on her lap. She had her wallet out, but she struggled with the purse's zipper that stayed open regardless of which way she zipped it. She gave up on the zipper and counted what little money she had. *Ummm, even less than I thought. If Mason's figured out a way to line his pockets, who am I to call him out on it?* She tossed the wallet back into her purse because there wasn't much sense counting what she didn't have.

She couldn't remember a time in her life when she considered doing anything like what Mason seemed to be doing, and let's face it, with two kids, she wasn't going to any time soon. Besides that, Stace simply didn't think she had the nerve to pull it off, even if she came up with some insane idea. *By the way, what day was it when Mason woke up with all this nerve and craziness?*

She'd never thought of Mason that way, but it certainly looked like he had all his thoughts in line. His plan was well under way. It was the details of that plan that bothered her the most. She knew she had told Mason she believed him, and for the most part she did, at least she wanted to. But logic had to step in at some point, and that was why her thoughts were siding with Reg and that detective guy, Warren. But an insurance scam without Jill? That didn't make any sense. There was simply no chance Mason would dive into something like that on his own. The dead doctor in a parking garage? She knew for sure that was nothing Mason would be involved in. So when the logic was not logical, she reverted back to believing Mason.

Of course, the more she thought about it, the more confused she got; but Stace was pretty sure about one thing. He was already in this deep enough, and nothing she could dream up would change anything. She still would be a stay-at-home mom, confined within her boundaries. She would still work like there was no tomorrow to keep everyone under her care as happy as she could. And even though Mason may be working a plan for something better, she would still have a shitty purse and an empty wallet.

She looked up at a rundown house across the street as Kyle rode by on a small, used up bicycle with training wheels. It was a simple reminder of what little she could provide.

***

Kyle's feet pounded the pedals to get the most he could out of this thing between his legs. When he turned back, the image of Stace grew farther and farther away which made him more and more motivated toward his sudden adventure away from home. He continued with his head down and legs pumping. He was determined to make a run for it while the warden was distracted. He approached a corner.

Kyle looked up from his handlebars and saw an old man. He approached Kyle from another street. He was alone and lost. At least to Kyle he was lost.

"Kyle, you're too far," Stace yelled.

He ignored her. Kyle tilted his head and watched the old man getting closer. Even though this man was older than anyone he had seen before, he seemed as comforting as the teddy bear that waited for him every night before bed.

"Kyle! You're driving me crazy," Stace shouted from way back at the porch.

"Hi, little boy." The old man knelt down to the level of Kyle on his bike. "Wouldn't you like to tell her to fuck off?" he said with a sheepish grin.

Kyle just watched him. He didn't know what that meant, but he managed a slight smile anyway.

"Problem is, saying that wouldn't really work out, right?"

Kyle was mesmerized by this cartoon character standing right in front of him and not on the TV like he would expect.

"There may be a day in your life when you'll be able to turn away and take off without a moment's notice. Wouldn't you like to forget your bike and soar through the air like you were born that way?" The old man chuckled. "You haven't got a clue, just like everyone else." He leaned forward and rubbed Kyle's hair."

The blue van pulled up to the corner.

Stace shouted, "*Kyle!*"

"Ahhh, there's my ride." He looked up, past Kyle. "Better go now, or she's gonna shit all over ya. Or me." He gave Kyle an eyebrow rising smile.

Kyle watched him walk toward the van and suddenly fall. Kyle got off his bike to help.

Another man appeared from the front of the van.

"*Kyle! Mason!*"

Kyle turned back to see Stace running like a hundred meter specialist. He looked at the old man who suddenly changed. His body tightened as if he was being held. He was on his knees with his head down. He took a few deep breaths. Suddenly, he snapped his head up. His hair was messed from the fall. His eyes were bugged.

Kyle was almost beside him when the other man stepped in. He calmly tried to get the old man moving.

***

Mason stepped onto the porch. He saw Stace running toward Kyle and a van—the blue van. He watched someone who looked like Dr. Harlow push away someone who looked like Andrew.

Mason bounded off the porch and launched into his

version of sidewalk track and field. He got closer and noticed it was Andrew and Dr. Harlow.

Andrew was ignoring Dr. Harlow's resistance. Stace was close now, and Mason closed in.

Andrew's eyes were on Mason as he rushed Dr. Harlow onto his feet and to the van. Dr. Harlow was watching Mason too. He tried to break free, but Andrew wouldn't let him go. Andrew got him into the van.

Mason approached Stace fast. She held on to Kyle. She was obviously flustered; not sure what to make of all this. Before Mason could get there, Andrew shut the door and rushed to the driver's door. Mason closed the gap. He got there just as the van pulled away.

Dr. Harlow shot Mason a deadly stare as they rounded the corner. Did he love him or hate him? The look on his face made it difficult for Mason to tell.

Stace said, "Jesus Christ, he's just a nice old man. I thought—." Mason saw her kneel down to Kyle and grab his shoulders. "Kyle, don't ever take off like that." She tried to get him to look at her, but he just watched the van drive off. She pulled him close; hugged him and looked at Mason.

Mason watched the van. He was focused like an angry wolf whose prey just got away.

"Mason, you're as white as when I saw you lying in your casket," Stace said.

Mason shook his head quickly and snapped back to reality. He saw Stace holding Kyle. He looked around at his old neighborhood. He rubbed his eyes to bring everything back into focus. *What the hell am I doing here?*

He sighed, watching where he last saw the van. "Yeah, sorry. Just a nice old man."

CHAPTER 25

If there was one thing Mason knew about the parents of young kids, it was not to get in the way when they were about to execute a day trip. Watching Stace and Reg in action was a sight worth witnessing, but trying to help was absolutely out of the question. He learned this from these two in the past, so he sat in the living room with Kyle and Emma while Stace and Reg engaged in full get out the door action.

"The cooler's ready, Reg." Mason watched her take off down the hallway. "Have you got money?"

Reg said, "Got it."

Mason could see him stacking a load of bags and jackets on top of the cooler sitting at the front door.

"And yes, I have money. Ask me after this though, and you won't like the answer." He picked up the cooler and everything else then barged his way through the door.

Stace sailed into the living room carrying a knapsack in one hand and swooped up Emma with the other. "Come on, Kyle," she said and made her way quickly to the front door without skipping a beat.

Kyle got up and looked at Mason. Mason's eyes shot to the door. He made a hand gesture to get him moving. The message was clear—go now, or shit would fly. Kyle got it, and he took off after Stace.

Mason sat alone. He didn't need to go with this family on their day trip or anywhere else for that matter. His best bet was to stay inside, out of trouble, until all of this blew away. Well, he knew everything wasn't just simply going to disappear, but staying put was definitely a better plan than living it up on family day.

Being alone for a while would actually be a good thing for Mason. It would give him some time to realign his thoughts about what he would do next. Which brought up an excellent point in Mason's mind. *What am I going to do next?*

Mason just then began to realize that when everyone abandoned his plan to escape, instead of bolting on his own, he should have at least reconsidered his strategy. Maybe he would have realized his plan had been leaked. That would have changed everything, or maybe it wouldn't have. Whatever the case, he now thought he should had never left without knowing exactly what he would do. For some reason he expected everything to work out. He thought the hardest part would be getting free, but it turned out his freedom was not an easy thing to secure. At least here, in this house, he was safe; so he thought this is where he should stay.

Despite that, he got up and walked to the front door. He stopped there. He watched Stace working at getting Emma and Kyle into the back seat of an older, four door Chevy. It was a task she simply had down to a fine art.

He saw Reg finish loading the cooler in the trunk. He cleared the jackets to the side and slammed the trunk shut.

"Reg, the bag," Stace yelled. The knapsack lay on the ground beside her.

"Oh, right. I got it." Reg popped the trunk open and rushed around to the door Stace's ass stuck out of.

Mason still watched from the front door.

"Let's go, Mason. The kids won't stay quiet," Stace hollered.

Reg grabbed the bag and looked back. "Come on, man. You can't just hide here. I know you still look like shit but it's better. At least you won't scare anyone." He smiled sarcastically, like a best friend would. "And one thing's for sure my dead buddy, you definitely need a life."

Mason reluctantly walked out the door.

"Look at that. The born again ogre's moving." Reg growled at the kids as he grabbed them through the door and over top of Stace. They screamed and giggled.

Still working in overdrive, Reg sped to the front door and locked it. He flung himself past Mason and into the driver's seat while Stace raced over to the passenger side. Within seconds, the doors were shut, everything in its spot, and everyone in their place. Everyone except Mason who stood beside the car still reluctant.

Reg powered down the window. He stuck his head out. "Fuck, man, this is as much for you as anyone else. Come on, it's gonna be a blast," he said with as much seriousness as Reg ever had to offer.

"I'm just thinking, Reg, I should probably just lay low at this point."

"How much lower can you get than riding Tipsy Tea Cups and Pop-a-Lot?"

Stace leaned over from her seat. "Mason, it'll do you good. Trust me."

He looked down and paused, knowing his argument was weak. "I'm just a little paranoid, that's all. With everything that's happened so far, there's no use taking chances. You guys know what I mean, right?"

"A guy who escapes from Doctor Death doesn't want to take chances." Reg looked cockeyed at Stace. "Now I've heard it all."

Mason sighed. He looked down while closing his eyes.

"Mommy, I gotta pee," Emma said.

Both Reg and Stace cringed.

Mason looked up wide-eyed. He looked at Reg and Stace who were both frozen, staring out the front window. In the back, Kyle squirmed while looking down at his crotch. Emma smiled huge. *Shit, responsibility's a bitch.*

Without being left much of a choice, Mason bolted into action. He squeezed his way past Kyle and took up a spot in the middle of the back seat. He took Emma's teddy bear and started moving it like a talking dummy. "What do you mean I can't see?" Emma and Kyle laughed. He reached with his other hand for the door.

As soon as he pulled the door shut, they were moving out the driveway and down the street.

CHAPTER 26

Mason listened to the chain turning as he sat with Stace in a roller coaster slowly climbing the hill. "Son of a bitch, Skillet. You must not have heard me when I said there was no damn way I would go on any of these things," Mason said as he white knuckled each hand grip.

"Oh, you big baby. Just don't puke," Stace said, looking over anxious to get this thing going.

The ride continued to climb. He looked down. "Shit. We're pissin' off the birds." *And I'm gonna be pissin' on them if this thing goes any higher.* He looked up to check how much higher they had to go.

"Look, Mason. Reg with the kids."

"That would mean I have to look down again, right? I don't think that's something I really want to do." Against his better judgment, he did it anyway. Reg had a huge smile on his face. He waved. Other than by size, it was hard to tell which one of the three was the adult.

"Bastard. It's his fault."

"Here we go, Mason. Put your hands up." Stace started to scream with her hands high in the air.

"Yeah, right." He looked straight ahead from the top. "Oh, shit." *Having died once already, you think I'd know better.*

"Hold your breath going down," Stace said but didn't follow her own advice. She screamed louder as the roller coaster sped down the steep hill.

Holding his breath was no longer a conscious decision. He couldn't help but think he should have fought harder against riding these rails. In a flash though, the hill was done. They continued into a loop forcing Mason to breathe, then another loop followed by two barrel roll twists. Just as Mason caught what little breath he had left, the ride made a sharp ninety degree turn forcing him to look over the side from ten stories up. Quickly it traveled over smaller hills and side winding turns until it finally came to a sudden stop.

Stace laughed loudly. She looked at Mason. "There, it's over."

Mason took a deep breath and smiled. He looked straight ahead. "Cool," he said, not really meaning it; but it was kinda fun.

"Wanna go again?"

"I think I already went." He looked down at his crotch. "Whew. I'm fine. Now I'll sit on a bench."

"No way, man. We'll find another one."

He got out, and waiting was Reg with the kids. Reg smiled as big as the clown who handed out balloons on the walkway behind them.

Mason said, "Now I know. The only reason I'm here is for added entertainment value."

"You got it, buddy." Reg grabbed Mason by the shoulders. "And now the crowd screams for more." He turned back to Kyle and Emma who were both yelling to get moving. "Hey, I saw a ride for the kids," Reg said with excitement.

***

Mason watched Reg sitting on a kiddy ride with barely enough room for Emma beside him. Kyle was in the seat ahead. Reg smiled and gave Emma a tickle while he looked back at Mason and Stace. The ride began with both kids laughing.

Reg played with Emma while the ride came close to Mason. "I think he's gonna bust a gut," Mason said.

"He's just a kid wearin' size forty two. I'm surprised they let him on," Stace replied.

"Who's gonna tell Reg he can't have more cake?"

Stace laughed with pride. "I remember you guys lifting weights all the time. He was a rock."

"Are you kiddin'? He was a God. When did he stop lifting?" *Like I don't know the answer to that.*

Stace looked at Mason. "He took it hard you know."

Mason turned with his back to the ride. "I've always thought cancer was punishment for betraying my best friend." Actually, Mason hadn't thought about this for a long time. When he got the news he had cancer though, it consumed him.

Stace turned away and watched the ride. "I'm glad you're back, Mason. I really missed you too. The hardest part was not being able to show it."

Mason watched her. He saw the hurt still in her eyes as she watched Reg and the kids. He knew the confusion she must be feeling. "So after I died..." He was taken back a bit by actually having said that out loud. "What did you guys do?"

"Well, Reg kept it all inside which forced me to do the same. I think if either of us had talked more, things would have been a lot better, but that never happened. I just got busier with the kids and around the house, and Reg got fat," she said, watching them on the ride. "Actually, since you've come back, we've talked a whole lot about you and us. It's good between me and Reg now."

"It's hard to believe you two ever had any issues." *Despite, of course, the part that involves me and you.*

"Well, we do, but you're gonna solve all of that, right?" she said with an uplifting smile.

"Ahhh, so it sounds like the man upstairs was done with me but not you two, so he sent me back as your guardian angel or something." *Talk about irony.*

"I thought a crazy doctor was your savior?"

Mason raised his eyebrows. "Harlow?" He shook his head. "That fucker is far from God."

"But according to you he's playing the part."

"Not really. I was never actually dead. Purify just cured me. They injected me with my first Purify serum just before I was ready to call it a day. That would have been in the hospital, then I figure they swapped me for some poor sucker sometime after you saw me in the casket. Freaky thinking I was actually alive then isn't it?" He shook his head. "Then of course, Jill did whatever she did with whoever was supposed to be me."

"Mason, do you hear it the way we do? I'm not saying you're lying, and I truly believe something happened to you. But how do you expect anyone to believe this?"

Mason looked away from her and stared at the ground. "I know, at least now I know." *But it's the truth, so what am I supposed to do?* "My first reaction when I broke out was to go home; get family and friends behind me."

Stace turned to him. "We're on your side, Mason."

"Yeah, but where's Jill. What the fuck happened to Jill?"

"Jill turned against us too, right away. Even while planning the funeral. Reg thinks she got word about the money."

"She knew about the policy. She's the one who wanted me to buy it so much, and I forgot all about it. The payments came out every month, but I didn't even notice. How the fuck do ya figure," Mason said while shaking his head.

"Well, that happens. We all lose track."

"Fuckin' smart talking insurance guy came over and had

her eating up every word he said."

"And just like the Mason Bushing I know so well, you did it," Stace said almost as if to lecture him. "Reg thinks she started planning and thought we would be all over her for some of the loot, as he put it."

Mason noticed the ride winding down.

"As soon as it paid out, she was gone. She had everything moved out of the house and left it empty. It has never even been put up for sale."

Mason shook his head. "I wonder where all my stuff is? That Fillmore guy said to get an address. It's already my place, and she wouldn't dare challenge it anyway." *How's that for a plan right off the top of my head.*

Stace touched his face to get him to look at her. "Stay with us, Mason. I want you to stay with us."

Mason wasn't sure what to make of that. She had just said things were going well with Reg. "You don't need me in the way."

"But I want to help you figure all of this out. I want you—"

"You guys remember you're in an amusement park, right? A place to amuse," Reg said.

Mason's head snapped up. Reg stood there holding Kyle's and Emma's hand. Mason stepped back as Stace instantly took on her mother role.

"Looks like Mom's tryin' to get Uncle Mason's laundry done," Reg said.

Stace knelt down to the kids. "Hey, guys. Was that a

blast?" She took them both in her arms.

Mason did his best to avoid the whole family thing, but Reg pulled him in by the shoulder. They started walking away from the ride.

"She'll get your head straight, pal. She's got lots of practice working on mine, and look at me now. I'm a believer," Reg said.

***

Mason walked with Reg along a crowded sidewalk, toward the midway. Stace was a bit ahead of them pushing Emma in a rented stroller. Mason looked up to see Kyle sitting proud on top of Reg's shoulders. It was getting dark. The lights from the midway shined with excitement.

Reg stopped to watch a carny show another guy how to throw a baseball into a wicker basket. "Come on. Give it a try," the carny said. The guy walked away. "How about you, big guy? Show the kid how it's done." Mason knew he had his next fish. Reg was pretty much already in the boat. "Here, I'll show you how." The carny stepped with one leg over the barrier already carrying two balls. He effortlessly tossed a ball which stayed in the basket. He looked back to Reg. "That's it. Simple."

He looked directly at Mason. "You too, man. Just toss it lightly, hit the rim, and it's done." He did it again—no problem. He held two balls up for either of them.

Mason backed away shaking his head. He turned to see

Stace watching too. Reg was reluctant to leave, so the carny zoned in on him. "Get down here low, toss it light–rim, and it's in." He grabbed another ball, and two balls were suddenly in Reg's face again.

Stace said, "Come on, Reg, let's go."

Reg ignored her; he was thinking. He slowly took Kyle from his shoulders and dug into his pocket.

"Ahhh, Reg, come on. Nothing you do has anything remotely to do with the word light."

Reg passed the carny a five dollar bill. "I know." The carny pocketed it and gave him the balls which Reg immediately passed back to Mason.

Mason backed away with his hands up. "No, no, no chance of that. There are kids here to impress."

Reg looked back at both Kyle and Emma. Stace gave him the all clear sign with her hand. Reg turned back to the basket—his imminent challenge with Kyle beside him watching. Reg bent down. He practiced the lightly thing. He tossed it, but the ball didn't even hit the basket.

Mason laughed, but that didn't seem to bother Reg at all. He still had one ball. He started aiming. He swung his arm a few times. The carny showed him again—simple. Reg aimed the ball again. He tossed it. It missed the rim. It went straight in the basket and bounced right back out.

Mason laughed again. He looked at Stace beside him laughing too. Reg reached back into his pocket.

***

Mason stood with Reg and the kids behind Stace who was poised with a soft mallet in front of a Whack-A-Mole game. "Three, two, one." She started hammering with the precision of a sharp shooter. Focused, determined; not a single whack missed its target. Mason watched the counter clicking consistently until the light on top of her machine started flashing and ringing. She jumped for joy and picked up Emma, so she could pick out a teddy bear. She gave Reg a superiority look and nudged past him.

Reg looked down to see Kyle, jealous. Mason tapped Reg on the shoulder and pointed.

***

With a rubber sledge hammer over Reg's head, Mason knew how this would turn out. Ding. Without hesitation, the mallet went over his head again and back down. Ding. Like he was born for this, up it went again; down; ding. Reg motioned to Kyle for him to choose a toy. He already had the large stuffed frog picked out.

***

Mason didn't feel out of place as he walked with the group along the midway. They were happy, enjoying each other—a family.

Kyle saw a huge merry-go-round. He ran toward it. Mason

started to go after him, but Stace got a jump start. She chased while pushing Emma in the stroller. "Kyle, wait." She caught him. "Don't," she pulled him back "you dare do that again." She made sure he paid attention. "Just like the other day, Kyle." He obeyed but Kyle still eyed his new found treasure.

"Stace, you go with them. I gotta find a washroom," Reg shouted.

"Me too, Skillet," Mason said.

Stace nodded and continued with Kyle and Emma toward the merry-go-round.

Mason went off with Reg in another direction. Reg said, "Glad you came?"

Mason nodded. "Yeah. You were right. Taking my mind off all the shit I've gotten myself into helps. Thanks, Reg."

Mason saw a washroom up ahead.

"We've got your back, man. You know that, right?"

"I do, Reg, and I appreciate it. This and taking me in. It makes me feel like I have the family I need." He nodded at Reg, sincerely, then he held up a fist. "And, by the way, you've got my debt too." He cautiously smiled, really having to know where Reg stood with this.

"Ha. Go figure I actually have someone who owes me money," Reg said proudly and produced his fist to complete the fist bump. "But since you're dead, it didn't cost me the house." He gave Mason a one arm man hug as they approached the washroom.

Mason curled his lips. "I'll get it back to you, Reg. I don't know how, but I swear I will one way or another," Mason said. He opened the washroom door for Reg.

"You'll do what you have to do." Reg went inside. "It's all good. Just don't go trying the dead thing again. Who knows how long I'll be waitin' if you do."

Mason watched him. *He still thinks I'm full of shit. And why shouldn't he? Even I'm beginning to wonder.*

"I may be a while, pal," Reg said, heading directly toward a stall.

"Don't hurt yourself. I'll wait outside." Mason stepped up to a urinal.

Two guys took a spot on each side of him, but Mason didn't pay attention to anyone else. He just took care of his business. He finished and stepped away. He walked to the sink and looked at himself while he washed his hands.

A guy turned on the water next to him. "Hey, Mason. Having fun?"

Mason looked at Steve. Quickly, he looked in the mirror. Andrew stood directly behind him.

Andrew leaned in, right beside Mason's ear. "Fun's over. Doctor Harlow has other plans."

Mason left the sink with the water running. He quickly went to the door. Andrew blocked him. He made a move to get past, but Steve pushed him through the door.

Mason was forced down a small outdoor path leading to the back of the washroom building. He reached the corner. Mason made another move to get away, but he was controlled by the other two. They turned him around. Dr. Harlow stood there.

"You're making it very hard for me, Mason." Dr. Harlow closed in, flanked by Andrew and Steve. "How are you making out on your own?"

"I'm fine," Mason said cautiously. "Better than all the other rats you have on lockdown, I'm sure." He searched with frantic eyes in all directions, but the place was all fenced in.

Dr. Harlow reached for him. Mason knocked his hand away. "I don't know why you're giving me so much trouble. Are you not grateful for me saving your life?"

"You keep me a prisoner with nut cases, and now I should be grateful?"

Now Mason was completely surrounded—Dr. Harlow in front; Andrew and Steve behind him at each side. He poised himself knowing what was coming. Typically, for Mason this was nothing he hadn't been able to handle; but now he was weak, and he knew it.

"I kept you separate from the mentally challenged. Another favor…"

"You used them to hide us, and you used me while you hid yourself; and whatever crazy thing it is you're doing. You can save my life all you want, but you'll never hold me down." He did a quick check at each side to be sure he knew exactly where Andrew and Steve were. He noticed Dr. Harlow getting closer. He felt Dr. Harlow touching his back.

"I have to, Mason."

Mason spun around quickly and knocked him away. Both Andrew and Steve closed in, but Dr. Harlow motioned frantically for them to hold back.

"If you didn't leave, Mason, things would be so much better," Dr. Harlow said then tried to see Mason's back again.

Mason realized he was after the exact spot Dr. Nichols found. He felt around himself but didn't take his eye off Dr. Harlow. The bump was back. He spun his head around to see it.

"There's something you don't know, Mason."

"What? What the fuck is this?"

Again, Mason knew Dr. Harlow was obnoxiously close and desperate to see. Mason pushed him away. "What the fuck have you done to me?" Mason yelled on the verge of panic.

"Only the most fantastic of all things you could possibly imagine, and now that I've seen it, I simply can't risk losing you again." Dr. Harlow showed him a compassionate but demented look.

"Well, I'm through with being your lab rat, so I guess you're just going to have to get used to it."

"I can't get used to losing what's so close to me, Mason. After all we've done to get this far. If I let you go, I may not find you again."

"Then report me missing. Try telling them one of your mental cases is on the loose."

"And risk all of my efforts, my working theory, my precious creations?" Dr. Harlow smiled with a look of ownership, power; insanity. "They had their chance, but they chose to toss me aside. Just like you, Mason. But unlike them, you belong to me."

Mason turned quickly and stepped back facing Andrew and Steve. He snapped back to Dr. Harlow.

Dr. Harlow's eyes glowed. He could see, in full view, the bump pulsing under Mason's shirt. "You need me, Mason. And I need you. It's time to come home," Dr. Harlow commanded.

"Harlow, the only way you'll get me out of here is on a stretcher."

Mason felt his shirt move. He watched Dr. Harlow's face fill with joy. Dr. Harlow grasped his hands together in front of him and his whistling started.

***

Reg opened the door of the stall, still in the process of doing up his pants. He walked to the counter. He put his hands under the tap that Mason left running then realized he never turned it on. He suspiciously tried to turn it off expecting it to keep running, but it shut off fine. He shrugged and took a quick look at himself in the mirror. *I guess some people just don't get to experience the thrill of paying water bills.*

***

Stace stood on the merry-go-round platform enjoying the peaceful ride despite being the thrill seeker she was. She held on to Emma who sat on a horse. That, and watching Kyle sitting on another horse moving up and down as the ride turned, was mostly the reason for her pleasure. There was also the fact that this was probably the first time today when she actually was relaxed. The ride continued and soft music filled the air. Stace felt like the merry-go-round could actually be the perfect place.

***

Mason was being backed up by Andrew and Steve. He cornered himself against the wall and a fence.

"It doesn't have to be this way, Mason," Dr. Harlow said.

"Fuckin' right it does." Mason prepared himself.

"But that's only because you refuse to trust me."

"No, Harlow, it's because you put your trust in the wrong corpse."

Mason looked at him. Dr. Harlow's eyes started to bulge. "And if I didn't, Mason?" His face exploded with anger. "*Where would you be now?*" Dr. Harlow flipped his hands like he was releasing his hounds. "*Where, Mason?*"

Mason spun back around. Andrew and Steve attacked.

"You'd be lying in the casket I took you from," Dr. Harlow said quietly, almost as though he said it to himself. "Surrounded in darkness—cold, damp darkness. But I saved you from that."

***

Reg stepped out from the washroom and walked toward the midway. He heard a noise behind him. He looked back but saw nothing along the path. He continued to the front of the building when he heard another noise.

***

Mason was pinned by Andrew and Steve when Reg appeared from the corner.

"Looks like I haven't forgotten what a fight sounds like." Reg smiled. "What the fuck, Mason. The trouble that surrounds you is as irritating as if someone just pissed on my leg."

"Hope you haven't forgotten what to do," Mason said urgently while he tried to keep Andrew and Steve at bay.

Reg stepped up and tossed Steve aside. "No chance of that, buddy, but shit man, save it for the bar."

***

The merry-go-round stopped. Stace lifted Emma off her horse, smiling and giggling with the joy of her young daughter.

Kyle cautiously began to get off the horse on his own. "Careful there, Kyle." Kyle continued without falling.

Stace jumped off the platform, with both kids eager for their next thrill.

***

While one-on-one with Steve, Mason controlled the situation easily. He landed two right hooks in a row sending Steve crashing against the fence. Mason waited for a response. There was none. He looked behind him to see Reg working with artistic ability as he easily handled Andrew.

After a flurry of punishment, Reg executed a crushing blow sending Andrew to the ground like his hands were in his pockets. Reg turned to look for Mason who was still watching him.

Reg backed up, moving closer to Dr. Harlow. "Ready to finish this, Mason?" Reg said as he straightened up for the final round. He motioned to Steve who struggled to keep himself upright against the fence.

Mason saw Dr. Harlow reach into his pocket. "Reg, behind you."

Dr. Harlow took out a knife. He extended the blade while whistling as though nothing out of the ordinary was happening.

Reg took another step back.

Mason lunged for them. He shouted, "*Behind you, Reg!*"

Dr. Harlow's whistling stopped. Reg turned quickly, but Dr. Harlow buried the knife into his back. It wasn't much of a thrust, but it was enough. Reg arced in pain. Dr. Harlow withdrew the knife and quickly, with a surgeon's accuracy, slashed Reg's throat.

Mason screamed, "*No!*"

Blood poured. Reg fell lifelessly to the ground. Mason ran to him.

"*Someone help me! Holy shit, I need help*," Mason screamed. He hopelessly tried to stop the bleeding. "Someone, please," he pleaded. Blood sprayed out of Reg's carotid artery, quickly losing its surge with every heartbeat.

Dr. Harlow leaned down to Mason. "You have to stay calm, Mason. If you won't let me help, you have to stay calm." He put a sealed capsule in his hand. "This will help, Mason. There's something you don't know," he said then tried to pick up a whistling tune, but he was unable.

***

Stace was startled when two guys rushed past her, then an old man ran right into her. She heard Mason's cries for help. She was confused. She noticed others around her reacting, but no one went near the back of the building. Stace quickly picked up Kyle. She ran down the pathway pushing Emma.

Stace saw Reg lying on the ground. Mason frantically was trying to stop the bleeding. He pushed down on Reg's neck with both hands, but blood ran through his fingers like water rushing through tangled roots.

Stace screamed, "Oh my God. Reg!" She put Kyle down and rushed to Reg.

Mason looked up, covered in blood.

Stace threw herself in Mason's place and desperately tried to get a reaction. "Reg, Reg, look at me."

He was dead.

***

Mason moved away. Stace held Reg. She moaned with grief. She rocked with him and looked into his lifeless eyes. Mason just watched.

"Just one chance to bring him back. Please, God, just one," Stace desperately sobbed. She looked up at Mason—her tears mixed with smeared blood.

Mason turned away. He saw Kyle and Emma. They both stared at their tormented mother, holding their dead father.

CHAPTER 27

When Mason had woken up this particular day, it felt odd to him that the events of the past week didn't seem to be weighing very heavily on him. This had been so much unlike other mornings when he sat in bed, or whatever it was he found himself in, and wondered what would come next, when it would happen, and what he would do when it did. This morning, however, his mind had been clear. He knew what was on tap for the day, but he didn't want to go.

Now Mason sat in the back of a police car. He was trapped, again. This time in the parking lot of an amusement park of all places. He wondered what made him change his mind. He had no business going to this place, with this family. If he hadn't, all this shit with Dr. Harlow would have still been there; but it would have been for him to deal with, and him alone. The simple fact that no one has ever really believed his story should have sent him back on the road long before now, but no, he had to stick around because that was easier. Reg paid the price for his convenience, and his two kids would never really understand why their father died. *It's all on me. Why the fuck didn't I just stay dead?*

He looked out the window to see a large crowd watching a stretcher being pushed into an ambulance. It was no longer a question of what and when for this day, he was only left with figuring out how he would deal with being accused of murdering his best friend. So far, that dilemma was out of his control. The locked down car he sat in now was just another indication of Mason's fate. It was the same he had faced over and over since what was supposed to be his final fate.

He saw Stace holding Kyle and Emma who were witnessing the horror of losing their father as the ambulance doors shut. Even at their age, that traumatic event would be etched in their minds forever, Mason thought. He wanted to break free from this confinement and scream out his innocence for everyone to hear. He wanted to tell Kyle and Emma that their father died helping him. He wanted to hold Stace, assuring her Reg died from the hands of a madman. *But what good would it do? They all think I'm a liar, and now they fear me. I'm a murderer to them.*

Among many police cars surrounding the scene, he saw Warren's unmarked car come to a screeching halt. Mason watched him storm out of his car and start searching. A uniformed officer approached him. Warren produced his badge while his mouth moved rapidly and his eyes continued to search. Mason couldn't hear any of what Warren said, and he didn't have to. In a matter of seconds, the officer's finger pointed to the car Mason sat in, and Warren's rampage came his way.

Mason's thoughts of innocence suddenly vanished, and now he was consumed with the basic instinct of survival. There was no way out for Mason and no telling what this raged lawman was capable of.

Warren pulled the door open nearly ripping it off its hinges. He reached in and hauled Mason out throwing him to the ground. He came crashing down on Mason's back and pulled his head up, forcing him to watch his dead friend's family in grief. "You think you're gonna keep droppin' bodies on my lap without a price," he growled, inches from Mason's ear.

Stace looked up, clearly afraid of what she was seeing.

"Tell'em why. First a doctor who knows too much, now your best friend who got in the way."

Mason reached out, trying to get Stace's attention, but Warren's aggression was too much to ignore. She looked at him. She appeared as though she wanted to help.

Warren pounded Mason's arm into the pavement. "You slit her husband's throat then beg for her forgiveness? How pathetic does desperation get when you wear the shoes of Mason Bushing? Or are they Reg's shoes?"

"I didn't kill him," Mason pleaded. "I didn't kill anyone."

Stace looked away.

Warren grabbed him by the arm. He forced him up and

pinned him against a nearby police car. "Your fuckin' story's old, man. Change it, now."

"There was more than just me. Find someone else—"

Warren was infuriated. "Assault, insurance fraud, two counts of first degree murder—"

"There was a guy, Bob, and Mark from another state. I can't remember where—" Mason struggled, desperately fighting a losing battle. "Jim, an older guy and Hazel. Her last name was…"

Warren grabbed him again, and threw him toward the open door of the police car.

"Bob Robinson. He has a family. Tell them he's alive."

Warren's further aggression sent Mason flying into the back seat.

"If diggin' me up is no good, dig up Bob Robinson."

The door slammed shut.

Noise from outside was instantly cut off and replaced with high pitched screeching; the chain of the roller coaster clanging; deafening screams of joy. Cameras flashed at the window. Mason struggled with conflicting sounds of the midway, a merry-go-round, children's laughter, and Stace's screams.

He jumped as though something jabbed his back. His shirt began to pulsate around his shoulders. He looked around frantically and felt with his hand. He couldn't see, but he felt his skin crawling on his back.

Suddenly, the front door opened. Chaotic noise from outside flooded the car as reporters swarmed, trying to get a shot of the murderer. A cop jumped in and the reality of chatter over the intercom broke the hallucination.

Mason sat back, traumatized, and covered in sweat. He could feel the terror in his own eyes as the siren started and the police car peeled away.

CHAPTER 28

Andrew stepped out from the same door where Mason escaped. He didn't plunge into a dark drearyscape, he wasn't breathing heavily, and no one chased after him. He just carried two bags of trash that contained waste from those under siege. If those bags were searched with even the slightest scrutiny, they would reveal what was going on in this place of questionable intentions. But Andrew didn't care about any of that. To him it was just garbage, and like most things he did around here, he would deal with it at a very basic level.

Once outside, Andrew sighed with relief for being away from the urgency always present behind that door. Having to deal with captured patients and untested medical procedures made stress just part of the protocol. He knew the doctor he was working for, or worshiping really, wasn't able to operate in any other way. Andrew was actually driven by it too. He thought about the people stuck here, and that they were still alive because of this environment. He smiled slightly—a proud gesture that acknowledged himself as a major contributor. But getting away from it for a little bit didn't do him any harm. Even for this guy who got a thrill from pushing people deeper into despair, despite what their lives had already been through.

After the door closed, he put the bags down and took a second to enjoy the morning sun that illuminated the field Mason had fled into. When he looked at it, he thought of Mason. Even though it was just another field, there was a sense of freedom that rose from it. He could picture Mason running farther and farther away, until he was out of sight. Although Mason used to be Andrew's biggest problem, in many ways, he was inspired by Mason's fight for freedom. Andrew felt he could run into that field just like Mason had, right now, and never look back. But Andrew didn't feel threatened here, and the fact that Mason was gone made things a lot easier for him. So why leave? He knew he was in this for the greater good. He also knew if anyone could operate in this environment, create the threat necessary to achieve that goal, it was him.

He looked away from the field to the only other structure that occupied this vast space—the larger building that cast this building in its shadows. It was its active appearance that gave the smaller one its innocence, almost like a storage house or some type of overflow area. Both buildings were not far apart. The only thing separating them was pavement that he thought was once used as a recreation area, evident from two poles for basketball backboards.

With nothing else to obstruct his view, he focused on blinded windows with outside screens and bars. They exposed a blur of activity in heavily lit rooms. Andrew knew this building's sole purpose was to distract from the activities he was involved in, but he also knew what went on behind those windows had some obscurities of their own.

Andrew picked up the bags and headed toward the windows. He was drawn to them, motivated by the fact that he couldn't see what happened in those rooms. He quickly approached the open, paved space which he knew would leave him exposed without the protection of the wall he walked beside. But he didn't care. He was alone now. Finally he would be able to find out what had eluded him for so long. As he approached the corner of the building, he raised the bags to conceal himself. He took another look at the windows then tossed the bags into a garbage container hidden around the corner.

He turned away thinking he didn't really care about activities he couldn't see, but now something else caught his eye—something he could see. It was the sewer grate Mason and Dr. Harlow had fought near. The grate sat up, not in its normal flush position with the pavement. Andrew headed toward it wondering who could be capable of moving the grate. It certainly couldn't be Dr. Harlow which left him considering Steve or one of the patients. But what would a patient be doing out here? And what would Steve be doing in the sewer? Whoever it was, he was unaware of what was going on, and that bothered him. He bent down to look into the depths the grate covered then looked back to the windows of the larger building. He thought for a second then glanced at the field. He turned to the door he came from, and despite some conflicting thoughts, he decided it wasn't worth worrying about. He kicked the grate back into its correct place and went to the door.

Andrew walked down a flight of stairs littered with leaves and debris then continued down a hall to another door. He opened it which exposed a small, dingy supply room. He saw Steve working in front of shelving secured to one of the walls. The other wall supported more shelves, filled with personal and medical supplies, but where Steve worked was much different. These shelves contained rollout trays of vials filled with liquid that displayed various color gradients from blood red to midnight black. Andrew stared at a few trays, including the one Steve had pulled out. It showed the full color range. Others started at blood red and ended somewhere in the greys.

Andrew came up from behind Steve, but he didn't startle him because of the small room size. "Nice to finally see some of the dark shit," Andrew said as he pulled out a tray and ran his finger along the row of vials that showed the full spectrum.

"Purify black? Yes it is," Steve said with a victorious smile. He held up a vial. He shook it a bit showing the rich, black liquid inside. This was obviously a prize for Steve, but for

Andrew, it just verified what they were doing and provided proof it could be done. Steve stuck a label on the vial. Andrew read it—*Purify 13 – tst 21, Pos.*

Andrew looked back at the tray he had been examining. It started with a vial labeled, *Purify 8 – Serum* and contained liquid that was midnight black. He picked out another lined up behind it full of blood red liquid and labeled, *Purify 8 - tst 2, Pos.* He put it back and at the end of that row, he plucked another filled with midnight black liquid labeled, *Purify 8 - tst 51, PURIFIED.* "Is this our fugitive?"

Steve looked up. "Purify 8?" He nodded. "Mason in a vial."

"So he's gonna have company soon?" Andrew said as he watched Steve finish up with the Purify 13 row.

"And he's not even here to say hello."

"I don't get it," Andrew said while looking at the tray with a puzzled look. "Why did Mason take so long, but this new one, like, she just got here?"

Steve pulled out two more trays. "Same for all of them."

Andrew looked at one of the trays that contained ten vials. The other held more than Mason's tray.

"It's like they're all on random timelines." Steve shook his head. "He either knows exactly what he's doing, or he's having a hell of a hard time figuring it out." Steve pushed those trays back into their secure position and pulled out another in a rack farther away. "At least they're better off than these guys."

Andrew examined all the vials in this tray. They started off filled with black liquid, then blood red, but they all ended up somewhere off the color chart. Steve pulled out another tray then another. Andrew picked out a vial with dark purple liquid and read the label—*Purify BD - tst 21, FAILED*. He took another with light green liquid labeled, *Purify DH - tst 44, FAILED*. He held it up to the light. "I think I remember this guy." He chuckled as he took a closer look.

Steve said, "You better hope he doesn't remember you." He took the vial from Andrew and placed it back then pushed in all the trays.

Andrew shrugged it off and headed toward the door. He turned back before opening it. "Are you saying I leave a lasting impression?"

"I'm saying if you meet again, the impression he leaves physically will likely last forever."

Andrew took a second to let that sink in, but he didn't get it. He gave Steve a squeamish smile and left.

He continued down a grungy hallway and entered a common room. Three men and a woman lay on decrepit, cot-like hospital beds while a movie played on a small, portable television sitting in what should have been a desolate corner. Andrew walked toward another door, trying to ignore everyone.

Andrew turned when Bob Robinson sat up in his bed. He wanted to laugh at Bob's shocking red hair and a mouth that always smiled, but he could sense this was about to be a serious moment.

"Hey," Bob said.

Andrew kept moving to the door.

"Hey, hey, Andrew. When we gettin' out of here? You can't just leave us like rats in the cellar."

"It's not my call, Bob. You know that. Ask Harlow. He put you here. He's the one who'll set you free." Andrew took keys from his pocket. He tried to avoid eye contact. "Well, not exactly free." He turned back to the door.

"And that's exactly why I'm after you. He probably doesn't even remember who we are. As to where we are? Forget about it."

Andrew could hear Bob get up, and the television go silent. He looked from the door while fumbling through the keys. One of the men had sat up and was kicking his legs over the edge of his bed. Another man tossed the remote aside. "Are you kidding? You're his prized possessions." Andrew smiled knowing he couldn't be farther from the truth. He decided eye to eye contact was now necessary.

"The prizes, he keeps under lock and key," Bob said, focusing on the keys in Andrew's hand. "We, on the other hand, are only his misfit toys." Bob started making his way toward Andrew, but stopped with his hands up as if to say they were all on the same side. He paced down the row of beds instead.

"Ahhh, poor Bobby. Don't worry, you're all locked in, I mean tucked in down here too," Andrew said with full intentions of leaving a patronizing effect.

The man sitting on the edge of his bed turned and gave Andrew a fierce look. Andrew knew he was by far the oldest in the room, and he also knew this guy feared him—he had seen the wrath of Andrew before. The woman, Hazel, jumped beside and rubbed his arm, calming him.

Bob stopped pacing and sighed. "But we shouldn't be. At least not down here."

"Well, Bob, just who should we blame for that? Wasn't it you who was supposed to keep the king of the misfits locked up with the keys in question?" Andrew responded.

"And a very capable guy got away. How is that my fault?"

"It's your fault because it was your plan to go along with him instead of mine to lock him up with more locks and more keys."

"So a plan fails and we pay?"

"Yes, Bob, we all pay. Have you noticed that I have to be down here too? I just came from outside, but I came back here. Why do you think I did that, Bob? Anyone?" Andrew waited for an answer.

The room was quiet. Andrew's stare at Bob shamed him enough, forcing him to look away. Bob looked back to the others, then he looked down. Andrew nodded realizing everything was under control here. He knew they all understood these steps were necessary in case the outside, where Mason was, got too close to what they did down here.

"That's right. Only one of us didn't feel this way, and trust me, the grass isn't all that green for our friend Mason."

"You've seen him?" Hazel turned sharply to Andrew.

Andrew chuckled. "Oh yeah, I've seen him. I saw him trying to recruit his buddy into this fancy little program here.

He must have forgotten that Purify doesn't work on trauma."

"But he's alive, right?"

"If you think he's going to rescue you from the fierce doctor, you're wrong," Andrew said while scratching his head.

"It's starting to look like he's the only hope we've got," she said.

"So you're losing confidence in the one person who didn't lose hope in you?" Andrew shook his head. He didn't really understand what the complaining was all about. "Look, you're all alive when you should be dead, right?" He paused to let that sink in. "Yeah, that's right, dead, like the guy who took one drag too many. Like the nice lady who just couldn't say no to her last puff pastry pinwheel cookie. Like everyone else who got to fill the shiny coffin bought on special order just for them. The man inside that room is who you have to thank. If you want to betray him, then Mason's your man. If not, then you're stuck down here in the cellar, because of your man, Mason."

The room was silent again. Andrew turned back to the door and the keys.

"That's all fine, Andrew, but where's the silver lining? Mason didn't see an end to this, and all that's being said here is, hey, we're having a little trouble finding it too," Bob said.

Andrew opened the door and looked in. "Don't worry, things will change. Soon, I'm sure."

Andrew stepped through the doorway, pulled the door shut, and locked it. He turned to the procedure room where

Dr. Harlow was in great pursuit of something. It was hard to tell just what the hell he was doing, partially because the room was a complete mess, but mostly because he wasn't acting much out of the ordinary. Obscurity was nothing unusual around here, but one thing Andrew knew for sure— Dr. Harlow was focused on something. When that happened, it would continue to be a problem until he either solved it or something else bigger, in Dr. Harlow's mind, came along.

Andrew bent down to Dr. Harlow's level, a little apprehensive about getting down and dirty with layers of dust, dirt, and dried bloodstains. Dr. Harlow was on his knees looking under a table with cables draping down from it like a teckie tablecloth. Andrew scanned the area looking for the problem. Dr. Harlow swung his arm back in Andrew's face holding an opened jar of peanut butter. Andrew wasn't sure what he should do. It was almost as if Dr. Harlow was offering him some. Then, Dr. Harlow snapped his head back with a steak knife covering his mouth, like a raised finger.

"Shhh," Dr. Harlow whispered as though any noise would set something off with disastrous results.

Andrew thought he knew what the problem was, and Dr. Harlow was right. Disaster would follow if it wasn't dealt with correctly, right now. He slid his hand forward. "Give me the remote," Andrew said calmly. He closed his eyes thinking the remote would be thrown at him any second.

Dr. Harlow passed him the peanut butter. He pointed to a triggered mouse trap on the floor at the end of the table, but he kept his eye on his target.

Andrew was confused. He focused on what Dr. Harlow looked so intensely at. It was a package of C4 mounted to the wall at the corner of the room. Then he noticed beside the package, a small, brown mouse had itself nuzzled in, desperately trying to hide from the crazy eyed monster pursuing him.

Before Andrew could react, Dr. Harlow held the knife by the blade. With a flick of his wrist, he let it go. It toppled end over end, miraculously through the cables, and stuck into the wall right beside the C4, missing it. It missed the mouse too, which scurried off for another hiding spot.

Andrew watched it travel quickly along a cable connected to the explosive, which took it to another paint peeled wall and another mounted C4 pack. Dr. Harlow followed it also. He was in front of Andrew and obsessed in a covert position. The mouse shot over the pack and fled into a dark corner.

Dr. Harlow chased it and popped up between two hospital beds, both with a slew of medical equipment connected to a patient in each. Andrew saw Dave in one and Linda in the other. Both were unconscious—coma like—but the active equipment showed their lives were supported.

Andrew stood up, still recovering from the C4 scare. He held on to another bed that was empty but hadn't always been. He noticed it covered with messed up sheets, stained with splattered blood and black liquid.

"The door! Secure the door," Dr. Harlow commanded.

Andrew nodded slowly. He knew he had to find some way to calm the doctor down. He watched Dr. Harlow plow through some boxes, a rolling cart carrying stacked trays, an unused intravenous stand. This cleared a path to the mouse's newest destination. It scurried across the floor nearly running over Dr. Harlow's feet which sent him flying into the bed Andrew used for support.

Calmly, Andrew went to the door. He opened it a crack and the mouse fled for the wall, sped along it, and disappeared out the door.

Andrew took a deep breath. He looked around the room to be sure everything was intact. He looked at Linda and Dave, hoping they were still near dead. He looked at Dr. Harlow to be sure he was still... Dr. Harlow.

Suddenly, a screech came from the other room. Chaotic activity followed. Andrew didn't move, but Dr. Harlow went to the door, shut it, and turned to Andrew. "Why isn't Mason here?" Dr. Harlow stared Andrew down. He obviously expected an answer as if nothing else mattered.

"Mason?" Andrew said, shocked over the fact that almost blowing up this whole operation, and everyone involved in it, seemed to instantly disappear from Dr. Harlow's mind.

"He's running out of time out there. Tell me, just how do you plan to get my Mason back?"

***

Andrew barged into the supply room, shocking Steve who carefully poured black liquid into a tabletop sealed capsule filling machine. "Let's go," Andrew commanded as he stormed through the room to the other door.

"What? Where?" Steve said, surprised by the urgency.

Andrew impatiently held the door while he watched Steve stop pouring. "Mason's been out there long enough. Any longer and this whole place will go missing, off the face of this earth."

"Mason? Shouldn't he be dealing with murder charges now? We'll never get anywhere near him," Steve said.

"Then we'll go for the next best thing."

CHAPTER 29

Steve thought that running surveillance in an upscale neighborhood in Rocksbrough wasn't what he should be doing for Dr. Harlow's underground experiment. The unauthorized part, the testing on humans part, the playing God part never deterred him from getting involved. In fact, he considered these things exciting and were probably the main reasons he had gotten his hands wet, very wet, in the first place. It was really just his youth that hadn't let him see beyond this thrill seeking experience. That same youth allowed him to sit in a beat up, blue van trying to figure out how he was going to kidnap some chick in broad daylight. But he was tasked with this challenge, so his young mind told him to do it.

Steve remembered coming to Dr. Harlow first as a Nursing Assistant in the main building's Psychiatric

Evaluation and Assessment Center. The Purify program had been in its early stages back then. Steve was young and naive enough to be totally taken in by what Dr. Harlow was doing. He figured something had been a little odd about the program's validity and the doctor administering it, but the program had a title. It had support from those who hired him, and it appeared to be funded. What could go wrong? He may have been apprehensive at first, but soon he was in too deep to care.

***

Andrew, on the other hand, watched the front door of Jill's house intently. He had no concern for what he was about to do since he always ignored the criminal side of things. He thought about Dr. Harlow's orders to get Mason back, and this is what he came up with. In Andrew's mind, he would do anything to impress the great doctor. He knew he was only a driver, but from the beginning he had always presented himself as someone who wanted very much to deliver for Dr. Harlow.

He knew she was in the exact house they watched. He also knew that busting in would set off alarms, and dogs, and neighbors, and whatever else they weren't prepared to handle under these rushed conditions. So he sat and watched—waited for the door to open. He figured Jill would eventually come out alone, jump in her car, and leave. Which is exactly what she did, so he started the van and followed.

***

Jill stepped out from the main doors of a Rocksbrough Shopping Center with enough bags for at least one store to call the day a success. She stopped on the sidewalk to rummage through her handbag. Without dropping anything, she pulled out her keys then walked straight into slow moving traffic. It was surprising she even realized there was a curb to step off. A car halted to a sudden stop. She saw it, but she didn't look up or even miss a step.

***

Andrew watched her from the van moving slowly behind the car. He turned into the lane Jill walked down. He saw her Mustang parked up ahead with the top down. He continued slowly, making it look like the van was waiting to take her spot. She approached her car and made a motion to throw her bags into the back seat. Andrew pulled the van right beside her and stopped suddenly.

***

At a corner, Steve opened the side door while the van turned with a slight squeal. He threw the shopping bags out before he slid the door shut.

CHAPTER 30

Rocksbrough Police Department's cellar seemed to be the place of choice for Mason to recover from his beatings. The previous one had been physical. Now he dealt with the mental kicking he got from Reg's death. He felt the weight of everything crashing down on him—the loss of his best friend, the kids losing their dad, not knowing what Stace thought, and that Warren guy who seemed determined to pin his ass for this and everything else. The longer this went on, the more it looked like there was no way out. All he could do now was watch the bars in front of him and wait for the next thing to hammer him into the ground where he should have been in the first place. Despite all of that, he couldn't help but try to think of a solution, but the faint sound of some irritating noise kept breaking his train of thought. Every time he tried, it just led to more failure and that damn sound.

Frustrated, he jumped up from the cot and lunged at the bars with a growl as though some superpowers would break him free. He rattled the cage to no avail.

The desk officer turned, pissed off from the disturbance. "Easy now, Robotron. If your plan to scare me out of here works, all the forces of justice will take aim on this place and bring you down with their mighty powers." He smiled and showed his portable PlayStation which was responsible for the annoying sound.

Warren opened the door to the detainment area. The desk officer handed him a key and gave Mason a look of superior thought power, supported by a finger tap to his temple. He mouthed *forces of justice* with an arrogant smile.

Warren walked toward Mason's cell. He flirted with the key in an obvious ploy to tempt Mason into thinking something good would happen. "I'm not quite sure how to proceed, Mason." He held up a file folder.

Mason turned away and sat back down on the cot. He remembered Warren's style in the interrogation room and realized he was about to be played again.

"What do you think's in the envelope, Mason?"

"Probably your pink slip for fucking up so badly on this one." He never looked up, but he could see Warren nonetheless. "And it's not an envelope."

Warren looked at the file folder. "Nope, it's not an envelope. And it's not my walkin' papers either." He stepped away pocketing the key. He grabbed a nearby chair and slid it up to the barred door. He sat with the file folder held out flat on his palm. "This is your future, Mason Bushing. It sums up everything that has happened recently in a nice little bundle. It has the potential to nail down your future into a simple eight by ten frame with decorative bars for a lasting effect."

Mason sighed. *Just what I thought.* "How about you try playing with yourself, and leave me out of your little fuckin' fantasy game?"

"Trust me, Mason, this is no game." He opened the folder and held up the first piece of paper.

Mason looked at it realizing Warren was probably not exaggerating much. This time had to come. He knew this guy kept count, and it looked like the total was hidden somewhere in that stack.

"Charge number one: Assaulting a police officer. You're a lucky man on this one, Mason." He pointed to a highlighted comment indicating *officer assaulted declined to press charges.* "He felt he got enough of you already, and our health plan bought him a new tooth, so he's not complaining." Warren shrugged as if to indicate he wasn't sure he would do the same.

Mason looked around the cell and settled on looking at the floor but definitely not Warren. "How long is this going to take?"

"Charge number two: Assault and Battery. Two charges here. The threat of beating the shit out of Tom Simpson and actually doing it."

"I never threatened him."

Warren chuckled. "You know what's really funny here, Mason? We asked him if he wanted to press charges, and he said to just give him ten minutes with you. I couldn't believe my fuckin' ears. He wants ten minutes with the guy who nearly comatosted him in two." Warren shook his head. "So I'm considering this one dropped too, mostly because I refuse to deal with a dumb fuck like that."

Mason looked up, straight at Warren. "Comatosted isn't a word." *Dumb fuck.*

Warren stared back then closed his eyes. He reopened them and held up another piece of paper. "Number three: Fraud. From a criminal perspective, you can say you are whoever you want to say you are; but when there's a million bucks involved, we get a little squeamish. We're gonna put this one aside for a bit, because Jill's got me all fucked up here. You too I think." He looked at Mason a little strange.

Mason knew what was coming next. *This is when the bars close in.*

"And of course, the last two take the curtain. Two counts of murder in the first degree. Dr. Nickolas Nichols." Warren looked up for Mason's reaction.

He had none. He didn't find the name, or anything, even remotely funny.

"And Mr. Reginald Walker."

Mason sighed and Warren showed respect for that.

"It's hard when you lose someone close, Mason. I know. I lost my wife, but let me make this perfectly clear. You're showing motive for both these murders, and you're my only suspect. The District Attorney is working on it as we speak, and I'm sure charges will be laid no later than the end of the week."

"I get a lawyer, right?"

"Of course. You've also got someone else. Stace…"

Mason's head popped up. His eyes were bright.

"She's covering your ass for the doctor, and she insists there's no way you could have killed her husband. I have to tell you though, none of us are convinced. We think she's acting out of not wanting to lose both of you." Warren got up and pushed the chair back. He fumbled through his pocket for the key. "Come on. We're going for a walk," Warren said.

Not wanting to lose both of you? How does he know about me and Stace? "Where?" He shook his head. *A walk? What do you mean we're going for a walk?* "Where, are we going?"

"I need to see what you think about something."

CHAPTER 31

Mason sat in the back seat while Warren's unmarked police car pulled into the entrance of Rocksbrough Cemetery. It crept along the driveway, past the office building, and past the parking lot without stopping.

Mason hadn't said a word during the ride, but the whole time he couldn't stop trying to figure out what was going on. Now that they were at a cemetery, he figured he should know, but he was still confused.

The car continued along a narrow cemetery road then stopped. "Call me a fuckin' idiot."

Really, to your face?

"And believe me, they're sayin' worse for requesting this little field trip."

Finally, someone sees the light.

"But your fairy tale seems to be hangin' on a desperate

piece of evidence, and I'm a sucker for details."

"Dot-n-cross kinda guy, right?"

"Nice, Mason. You're paying attention." Warren nodded in the rearview with a big smile.

Fuckin' idiot. "I'm also paying attention to the fact that I'm no longer charged with anything." He waited for a response.

Warren sighed. "Figure I'm doing you a favor protecting you from yourself. Where would you go anyway?"

Mason realized he was actually free to leave right then and there.

"Actually, it's the only reason I got you a day pass, so I brought you here to show what you're up against," Warren said. He opened his door, got out, and quickly opened the door for Mason.

Warren turned away. Mason could tell he was looking at the vast field of headstones broken up by trees and various sections of landscaping. The morning sun shone which Warren obviously enjoyed. He took in a deep breath of the freshly cut grass. Mason watched him walk into the field and stop in front of a headstone.

"Something about a place like this first thing in the morning. The innocence, the peacefulness, the honesty…" Warren turned back.

Mason watched him from beside the car. Reluctantly, he started to catch up. The uncertainty he felt was an understatement. Surely, Warren wasn't going to tell him about a mistake, and any minute now he would see his own headstone?

"Is there a place that gives you comfort, Mason?"

"Ahhh, not really," Mason said but he thought about how this would be it, if what happened next set him free.

"That's too bad. I think we need places like this in our lives. A place to reflect and remember." Warren took a few steps down an aisle of headstones. "In loving memory of Robert Donald Robinson, 1915 - 2010."

The slight moment of freedom in Mason's mind instantly vanished and was replaced with the familiar confusion he couldn't get away from.

Warren looked at Mason then beyond. "Bob lived a nice life. Your doctor—Harlow right—picked a ninety five year old to give it back to." Warren started to walk away. "A young guy like you I can see, but then you said Harlow was insane." He turned back since Mason didn't move. "You like baseball, Mason? I do. Strike one."

Shit. Mason could tell from Warren's sudden change in demeanor this wasn't set up to go in his favor. *But wait, I told him to dig up Bob Robinson. If he didn't find him, why would we be here?*

Warren jumped a few headstones and stopped two rows over. He planted a huge smile on Mason. "A short distance away we have another Robert (Bobby) Robinson. A much better choice for dear Doctor Harlow. 2005 - 2013. What's that, eight right? Seven, depending on the birthday he's now missing." Warren paused for a reaction. "Strike two."

Mason watched, unimpressed with being Warren's source of entertainment. He shook his head with another shimmer of hope vanishing away. He knew it was just a matter of time before he'd be back in the PD cellar.

"What's wrong, Mason? You look bummed."

Mason followed as Warren walked on.

"Sorry, but I couldn't resist. Three right here in the same registry. What are the odds?"

Mason saw the smile on Warren's face. *Fuck, man. You're killin' me here.* Mason couldn't believe he actually followed up on Bob Robinson—and he found him?

"Crazy shit some people do. They put a picture of poor old Bob right on the rock."

Mason slowed down. *A picture? What the...* Mason stopped, but Warren kept walking toward a headstone. Mason looked through the cemetery. He saw cruisers—one in the parking lot, and two on the street. He saw rows of headstones, a fence. It all started spinning.

Warren looked back from up ahead. "What's wrong?" Warren suddenly appeared very serious. "Just a few more steps. You can do it," he said.

Mason started walking again. Slowly at first, then urgently to the stone. He stared at it—the picture. Bob Robinson's eyes pierced his. He was a black man, not a red head with a huge smile.

Mason stood still, staring at the headstone. His legs buckled slightly.

Warren said, "And there it is. Strike three."

Mason regained his balance. He looked away, toward the parking lot. Police cars... He looked back to the grave site then the opposite direction. Headstones… He began to walk away from Warren.

"And he's off," Warren said.

Suddenly, Mason began to run.

"Like a spooked pony with no lead lines."

Mason looked back to see the cruisers taking off. Police officers on foot were in direct pursuit. Warren was right with them.

Mason ran through the landscape of symmetrical rows. He leaped over obstructing headstones. A chain link fence was ahead, blocking his only way out.

At the fence, he looked back to see Warren still moving and making up lost ground.

"Why run, Mason," Warren yelled. "Think about how those murder charges will look if you do."

Mason's distance advantage was gone.

"And how does it change if I don't?" Mason started to climb. He continued to the top and rolled over. He lost his grip and crashed to the ground. He stumbled to his feet.

It was a backyard he was trapped in. Ahead, there was another fence to get over. He leaped toward it and was over like it was not even there.

Now he was in another backyard. He frantically tried to get his bearings. There was an opening at the side of the house. He ran there.

Mason stopped suddenly in front of two blocking cruisers. He saw a park on the other side of the street and went for it. Squealing cruisers motivated him to keep moving.

Mason ran as fast as he could and within seconds, he moved at hyper speed. He was motivated sure, but this wasn't just powered by desire. It was fueled with turbo adrenaline.

He headed for a ravine and the security of dense bush.

CHAPTER 32

Mason knew the police search crew had finally lost hope. He wondered what would have happened if they had stopped and stayed completely still. They would have heard nothing but the rustling leaves of trees, the trickle of water flowing in a small creek, and the unmistakable sound of heavy breathing.

Mason was in fact still here, buried deep in the decaying carcass of a large oak tree that had probably been lying on the ground for as long as it was upright. It was no wonder they couldn't find him because he couldn't even see himself. He was relieved they had failed to leave every rock, or tree, unturned which gave Mason his current freedom; but that was the least of his concerns. What happened after he settled here had completely taken over and required his absolute privacy. He thought that snooping eyes of annoying police officers would not have gone well with the convulsions, the blackouts, the deafening high pitched screeching in his ears, or the surging body parts. All of this had left Mason unaware of the massive search going on around him, but now he was calm, and they were gone. Just his heavy breathing remained.

Although Mason was alone, he thought his current troubles were likely not over, so he stayed still waiting for something else to contort in his body. He didn't know what the effects were, having just spent hours going through this process, but he knew Dr. Harlow did. That explained some of the doctor's strange actions, and his total obsession for Mason. He was now realizing the work Dr. Harlow was doing didn't just involve bringing people back from the dead. It was much more than that. He also realized Dr. Harlow was the farthest thing from the lunatic he always thought of him as. Sure, he was different and that came off as crazy, but it was because of what he was protecting. Mason realized now Dr. Harlow knew this would happen, and he knew how to control it, but Mason messed up the plan by leaving.

Why didn't he just tell me? Better yet, why didn't he leave me alone in the first place? Did he pick me out of some line up, or was I just some random selection of the day? But when Mason seriously thought about it, if he was taking people from a small town like Rocksbrough, it must have been simply a matter of who was next on the death list.

Mason remembered Dr. Harlow always pressing the point that they, all the patients, should have been grateful for him saving their lives, but he had never considered the fact that some people simply didn't want to be fucked with. Facing death or not, Mason was one of these people. From what he could tell, here in this cocoon-like hiding place, he was not even close to the kind of guy who could handle what was happening to him now. The thought of that chilled him, but he was far too confined to do anything about it. The cold dampness here did make him realize though, he had nothing on.

He stretched his hand against his leg and felt flesh—silky smooth flesh. His other hand was tucked in around the back of his neck. He felt up, and again, it was smooth; like his hand slid on clean ice. He realized he was experiencing other physical feelings. They were the same touching sensations he would normally get from his hands, but they came from other unrecognizable parts of his body. He wanted to resist the transition, but his body had taken over, like it was on auto pilot until his mind caught up and bought into the plan.

So what was next? He would eventually get out of here, and when he did, then what? Or was this a mind over matter thing? What if he was just laying here with his body all prepared for whatever, waiting for his mind to take over? What if his mind couldn't? Would he just stay here and rot like the tree that provided his cover? Whatever it was, there was nothing he could do about it because he couldn't move at all. Simply put, something would have to give, or rot would eventually settle in.

For the first time since Mason had escaped from Dr. Harlow, he realized he should have never left. Mason knew nothing about what was happening, and he couldn't have been more unprepared. The life he'd had before was now turned upside down, and that was really all he had ever wanted to get back from this experience. Now he would have to deal with this, and he had no idea where it would take him. Forget about the mess he had just left behind. Forget about Jill who didn't want him anymore. Forget about the affair he'd had with Stace, the wife of his best friend who had died because of him. But he wasn't ready to forget about all of that, and if he was ever able to get back to it, it would be from a totally different perspective.

He took a deep breath, cut short with another convulsion. This one was much less intense but still scared Mason, so he braced himself for more. He tried to see his hand, but it was no use. He could only go by the way he felt, and that seemed to be powerful. He thought after all he'd gone through, he should be feeling sick and ready to pass out, but it was the complete opposite. He wanted to get out of here and use that power, but the time wasn't right. Along with the power was a deeper sense of control which kept him here calm during this whole experience. So he stayed still and simply waited it out. What was happening had to finish, and he could tell at least physically, that would be soon.

He started to move whatever he could. He got a little movement from his right shoulder, then his hip. Within seconds a claustrophobic panic fell over him. He hadn't felt this before because he couldn't move at all, but now freedom was in sight, so the rush started to get the best of him. He controlled it with more heavy breathing and kept moving, getting the slightest movements from his foot, his knee, and his head. While he worked to move the hand near his leg, he felt something else familiar but not a body part. It was small, oval... It was the capsule Dr. Harlow had given him when Reg died.

Suddenly, he could move more. He pushed and squirmed, pulled and kicked. He busted up everything around him that held him so tight. He maneuvered himself from every body part, old and new. Finally, with a sudden surge of strength, he burst free of his confinement. Although he wanted to blast out of here, the control part kept him right where he was, and he just started breathing heavily again. *All in good time, all in good time.* But now he knew it was over. Now he knew he was completely different. Now he knew nothing held him back.

CHAPTER 33

Darkness, confinement, and disorientation consumed Mason during his first steps away from the fallen tree. He staggered and stumbled. He crashed through low lying trees and bushes; breaking branches and splashing through water, but he kept moving. He let out a howling cry of freedom. Then he stopped—silence.

Suddenly, he was moving again—controlled and deliberate. He knew destruction was within his capabilities, but there was nothing here to destroy, and he was much more focused anyway. Despite the dense bush, he plowed forward with nothing stopping him. He moved into a clearing where he saw a flash of his white flesh. Then he continued up a hill, flattening a path of overgrowth. He blasted out from the bush into a field.

He started moving toward a sparsely populated road when

he realized his legs were supported by larger ones. These strange appendages just followed his normal movement, but Mason was confused about what was now part of him. He moved faster, and they kept up, but they provided no assistance other than superior balance. He felt asphalt under his bare feet. He looked down to see the copying movement of two additional feet. With a lean to his right, the new right leg propelled him forward. It set him off balance which he tried to correct with his left leg. His weight shifted causing the new left leg to surge like the right one just had. It took him a few strides to get the synchronization and balance right, but soon he moved at an alarming rate.

With houses on one side and bush on the other, he tore up pavement that separated the two. His speed was incredible. He went full throttle along the long, straight road as though toying with his new found freedom. Suddenly, two small arms appeared below his normal arms. They supported a small wingspan that lifted him into flight. He hovered barely above the ground then touched down for more thrust. There was no slowing down. Ahead was nothing but open road, and there was no reason to stop.

Mason's increasing confidence meant more flight, each time higher and longer than the last. His weightlessness didn't come from a flapping wingspan or a buzzing membrane. It was kite like—an integrated part of his body.

Finally, he came to lights, but he had no intention of stopping. A touchdown was followed immediately with smooth aviation through a lightly traveled intersection. He watched himself step on the roof of a car leaving four human foot prints. Then he soared straight up.

He continued while slowly losing speed. At the top of the ascent, Mason held his position for a second, leaving himself weightless. He looked at city lights in the distance. Moonlight revealed his completely hairless body, four legs and four arms, two of which were webbed to his torso. He knew he wasn't a beast of the past, he was an evolution from Purify.

His fall sent him into a graceful descent which he leveled out before impact. He flew among cars, just above the pavement, with occasional touchdowns to maintain speed. In and out of traffic on a more heavily travelled road, he played with his abilities leaving metal havoc in his trail. He left this road for the rural wasteland he much preferred. Here he found the freedom he had been looking for, and with his new abilities, that freedom was at least some consolation for what he had gone through.

He sailed over hills and through farm fields. Mason didn't have any idea where he was, or where he was going, and he wasn't worried about it. Just the feeling of being in control was good enough. It definitely felt like his body was still running the show, but he was okay with that. He certainly wasn't ready to take over, and the fact that something else drove was reassuring to say the least.

Finally, he stopped on the upgrade of a dirt road. He didn't know the route he took to get here, but now he knew exactly where he was. With this new body came a new, heightened sense—instinct. It was instinct that also told him the freedom he just experienced would be short lived.

As he walked to the top of the road, Mason looked at himself—a slick, ripped creature of perfection. Beyond was a compound of buildings. He sat down and looked all around, then again at the buildings. He looked at his legs, then his arms. He rubbed his bald head and uncurled his lizard like tongue that held the sealed capsule Dr. Harlow gave him. He snapped it open with a bite. The black contents flowed into his mouth, some spilling over.

CHAPTER 34

Mason walked down the hill completely naked and hairless, but he was a normal human again. Although he moved with extreme confidence, he was terrified about what he would do if—when it happened again.

It was fine out here looking like this, or that, but having to live with it in society… Finding more of those capsules was only part of the answer. He simply had to learn how to control it. Dr. Harlow always told him to stay calm and breathe. So this is what that was all about, but for Mason there had to be something more permanent. He didn't want to be the main attraction of a midway sideshow. He didn't want to be the superhero kids like Kyle idolized with pajamas and matching bed sheets. He just wanted to be Mason, Mason Bushing. A factory worker, a loving husband, a caring friend—a normal human being.

Now he knew what Purify was all about and what Dr. Harlow was capable of. He knew why it was all secret, why he had been stolen from a casket, and why they wanted him back. He knew why the believers would kill for it. But he didn't know if he was capable of being its poster boy. Nevertheless, the decision had been made for him. Now he had to figure out how to deal with it.

There was only one person who could help him with that. He built it from the start, and he had taken Purify to where it was. Mason had always thought Dr. Harlow couldn't even help himself, so how the hell was he going to help him? But he had done this to Mason, and he would have to be the one to see him through it to the end. At least Dr. Harlow would have more of what got him back to normal. If this was Mason's future, that change agent may be just the thing that keeps him from living in a cave.

It all seemed crazy to Mason. After all he had been through—all Dr. Harlow had done to him. *Damn, this guy actually killed Reg.* But there was no question here and no decision to make. Like it or not, Dr. Harlow was God to Mason, and Mason needed him to finish what he created.

Everyone else still under his care seemed content with that. Why should Mason feel any different? But they were only dealing with being alive. Mason wondered if becoming something else would change their minds. *Probably not.* As dependencies go, once you're hooked, there's usually no turning back.

His pace was deliberately slow going down this hill. He

wasn't sure if he was ready to face what he so eagerly wanted to get away from. How would he even make it known he was here? Then he remembered his escape; the sudden storm that had erupted in his head. He had no idea if it would happen again but if it did, there would be no way out.

He stopped on the hill; he looked back to the road. *Can I do it myself?* He could just turn away, and find somewhere to start new. That's what he should have done in the first place. But it would never be that simple, and Mason knew it. Especially with these new developments. The decision came down to this: find a way to live as what he was, or end it right here. He thought hard. It was no different than where he'd been before all this started. He was given a shot, but it didn't work out. That's all. It was no more complicated than that. But it was more than death itself. This was about him doing it to himself—taking the life he had fought so hard for. It was a somber feeling for Mason, realizing how a person feels when they're considering taking their own life.

He stood on the hill. A light breeze cooled his naked body. He looked at the clear sky above him. It was dark for as far as he could see. No one could have painted a better picture of the end, but Mason was not the type of man who made decisions like this. He was a fighter even if the fight was already won. He battled on for the sake of the battle. He was first in line when the beer bottle broke. Maybe Dr. Harlow did pick the right person. *Maybe I should be the first survivor.*

His sights turned to the main building of the Psychiatric

Evaluation and Assessment Center. From where he was now, Mason couldn't even see the smaller building. He knew though, that it was the only place where he could survive. He also knew the secluded building full of secrets would be his final destination tonight.

CHAPTER 35

As Dr. Harlow worked hopelessly to move the empty bed away from trapped equipment, he relentlessly blamed these conditions on those who had stripped him of his medical license for conducting unethical drug tests on mentally ill patients. This was the reason for him being here, but it didn't keep him from staying current with modern medicine and being capable of running a small lab in the middle of nowhere. He stopped with the bed and smiled thinking about this. Sure, his ban from research and development years ago isolated him from his peers, but he had done just fine on his own with, up until this point, no one the wiser.

He knew his problems mostly had to do with old, broken down equipment and his general housekeeping skills. But as long as his stuff worked and current Purify case studies moved forward with positive results, he couldn't care less about any paper that allowed him to do this or any nurses who could provide useful help. It didn't matter if his machines had shiny, new cover plates; or if there were any dust bunnies in the corner.

Dr. Harlow did care about his patients though, at least the ones who were active in the Purify protocol. He remembered many of these people over the years, and although he wasn't particularly good at keeping track of them, he cared enough to definitely keep them at arm's reach. He especially cared about patients who could give him another positive test result. On this particular day, that patient was Linda.

She lay unconscious, with Dr. Harlow anxiously taking notes from what his diagnostic machines read out. He dodged back and forth between each side of the bed as though the machines competed against each other and he kept score. He looked up, frazzled, when Steve entered the room.

"Quick, Steve, quick." Dr. Harlow sprung to him and pulled him like a child showing his new found discovery. "Anytime now. I can feel her living right through me." He shook with an artificial chill. "My second…" He looked away, suddenly depressed. "Success." Dr. Harlow was instantly rejuvenated. "And we have Dave now too. Can you believe it?"

Steve stared back, appearing flustered by the sudden flurry of activity.

Dr. Harlow looked at Dave laying in another bed with many instruments connected to him. He wasn't interested the way he was with Linda, but they were both hooked up the same. He thought both were on their way to a successful rebirth. Since Dr. Harlow had lost Mason, and since he knew Mason was Purify positive, things around here were on a ramped up timeline to get more of what he'd lost. Of course, he hadn't forgotten about Mason, and he hadn't lost all hope in getting him back. Right now though, Dr. Harlow's focus was on Linda, so everything else just lingered in the background.

Dr. Harlow threw himself into a chair at a table full of computer monitors and just about everything else imaginable, used and useless. The chair rolled back, into a small C-4 plastic explosive bundle mounted on the wall. He looked at it but just pushed himself back to the table. He leaned over and ripped paper from a machine that continuously pushed out a small strip. Dr. Harlow looked beside the machine at Jill shaking in a corner. She was gagged and her hands were wrapped tight with duct tape. The look in her eyes showed nothing but fear and disbelief, but Dr. Harlow didn't care. He was confident she was secure, so he hurried back to Linda.

"There it is. Precisely where she should be." Dr. Harlow showed the printout to Steve. He turned back to Linda. "She'll be coming out any minute now."

"Do you want me to leave?" Steve said.

"No, stay. You'll witness a rebirth. Change ya forever." He continued monitoring while he whistled to ease the tension.

***

Mason approached the main building some distance away from the smaller one which was now visible. It was somewhat relieving to see, but he wasn't anxious to go there. He hadn't been noticed, but he knew each step closer was one less step before alarms would start ringing. Then, his head would scream. *Hey, look at the positive side. At least I won't have to risk some stranger opening the door to me standing there naked.*

He stopped walking, looked at the small building, and considered that. He realized there was a possibility Dr. Harlow wasn't even here. Mason had been gone for over a month. The risk of having him on the outside may have sent Dr. Harlow, and his band of medical wannabes, runnin' for higher, or lower, ground. Although the thought should have been a relief for Mason, it was much more terrifying. After all, the only reason he stood anywhere near these buildings was because he needed to meet his maker again. Finding out this whole operation was gone would only put him into a desperate search.

He kept walking along the wall and came up to a row of windows covered with wire mesh and metal bars. He approached them but couldn't see in because of closed blinds. He turned away and looked at the small building again, thinking it really didn't matter anyway. He had more pressing things to deal with. He stood there looking, but he didn't make a move toward the building. It was either because of wrong timing, or he wanted to talk himself out of it. He was not sure, but something kept him from moving.

Hold it a second. If Harlow's not here, I am… naked; and lights are on in there, meaning someone else is too. Maybe I should be thinking about some basic necessities. That made him look back to the windows. One had its blind partially open.

He bent over and looked in. Mason's eyes popped. His head snapped back, and he nearly fell. He was shocked beyond belief.

***

Linda rapidly began to move her eyes behind closed lids. She moved her hand slowly. Suddenly, she thrashed her head and opened her eyes wide. A blur of white light flooded in causing her to quickly shut them. Instantly, the feeling of reality overwhelmed her. It was so different from the feeling she had just moments ago.

The last thing Linda remembered was giving up. She had been stressed with each breath, deep and labored, not knowing which one would be her last. She remembered a nurse trying to calm her, but those efforts were useless. Linda's end was certain. It was just a matter of waiting it out. She had been counting down the breaths—not that one, so she took another. She remembered the sudden prick of a needle in the back of her hand. A warm flow washed from her hand, up her arm, and through her whole body which brought her to this moment.

With her eyes still shut, she reached over to react to the needle prick. Her hand got tangled in a web of wires, not there seconds ago. She thought the nurse would be able to help, so she slowly tried to open her eyes again.

She saw an old man looking over her, not the nurse she expected. That bothered her, but she also realized her breathing was not labored anymore. In fact, it was clear, instinctive, just like it should be. Her vision beyond the old man was blurred, then slowly, the room came into focus.

The old man smiled back at her. "Hi, Linda. Welcome back."

"Who are—where…"

She noticed him trying to keep his attention on her, but he also watched the monitor on the table that rolled out a strip of paper. It was blank. He checked it closely. He smiled back to her, extremely pleased.

"I'm Doctor Harlow. I'm sure—"

Suddenly, Linda's eyes flickered. She was drowsy. Her head waved as though she would faint even though she was lying down.

***

Mason recovered from his near fall and cautiously approached the window again. The blind blocked most of his vision, but he could see inside the room at a zoo of mistakes. He straightened up, shaking his head with both hands covering his eyes. He looked back to the smaller building then the window.

Inside, a few invalids slept but many provided continuous

resistance for two nurses who tried to keep order. Mason watched the nurses herd this wildness into a controlled group. The blinds blocked his view from seeing everything, so he looked closer which allowed him to focus between the blind veins.

A deformed man scratched his rippled back while he repeatedly opened and closed a closet door. A two headed woman plucked hair coming from her obvious dead head. Another nurse mopped puke while a deranged woman sat splashing in her pee.

Obviously, chaos was normal here. Mason knew exactly who was responsible for the pandemonium.

***

Dr. Harlow still stood beside Linda, but she was unconscious again. He quickly wrote down what displayed on the monitor beside her. He reached over and ripped the strip of paper that again produced a readout. The pleasure he just had was now completely gone. Frantically, he checked the monitor then back to the paper strip. He turned, desperate for the door.

Steve was in his way, but that didn't slow him down. Dr. Harlow saw Jill as he passed her, but he didn't stop for her either. He looked at the readouts he carried, studying data on the run. He stopped at the door. As he flung it open, he looked back at her. He pierced a stare at Steve. "I said I want Mason back. Here, now." He looked back to Jill. "Use her."

He left, slamming the door shut.

Dr. Harlow rushed through the common room as though no one was there. He knew everyone in the room heard the door. Before anyone could confront him, he watched Bob jump up and calmly distract the others, giving Dr. Harlow clear access to the other door.

Dr. Harlow went directly to the wall of vials in the supply room. He pulled out the tray labeled *Purify 13*. He stood there and examined the row of test samples considering what his next move should be. He hesitated but grabbed the first vial labeled, *Purify 13 - Serum*. He gulped then pocketed a syringe and a vial from a nearby shelf.

He quickly went to the table and the capsule filling machine. He grabbed a cup in front of it, shook it, verifying there were some capsules. He took one and left the rest.

***

Mason turned away totally defeated. He took a few steps toward the other building but stopped not knowing whether he should go. If he let Dr. Harlow continue, would he end up like that? But he already was really, and his version worked. *Rejects… They're Purify rejects.* As he started for the small building, he looked back to the window. Suddenly, Mason grabbed his head as though it was about to explode. He fell to his knees.

***

In the supply room, an alarm shattered the silence. Dr. Harlow stopped dead, as though frozen by what he was doing. His eyes lit up like a moon that just blew a fuse. He roared, "Andrew!"

He blasted through the door to the common room. Andrew was right there. He grabbed Andrew by the shoulders. "Mason's back. My Mason's come home."

***

Linda was fully awake and looking around this laboratory nightmare. She heard Dr. Harlow's joyous cries.

"And just in time," she heard him yell from somewhere beyond the door.

She tried to move then realized she was wired up like a homemade science experiment. She saw a man in the bed next to hers. He appeared to be in a coma. After more examination of the room, she realized someone else was tied up in the corner. She tried to call out to her, but her voice didn't work. She gulped and coughed. Even the cough was silent.

Linda saw Dr. Harlow and someone else at the opened door. Dr. Harlow snapped back against it, shutting the other person out. He seemed thrilled to witness her revitalization, but Linda panicked at the sight of him. She squirmed in the bed as he approached her. It looked like he was going to hug her or something. She thrashed over to her side ripping out most of the monitoring equipment. She tried to scream, but nothing came out.

Dr. Harlow yelled, "Andrew!"

Suddenly, the other guy grabbed her just as she was about to roll off the bed. He hauled her back onto it while she saw Dr. Harlow filling a syringe. Linda panicked under the force of being held down, and the threat of an old creep with a syringe as a weapon. From what she could tell, these two were as deadly as the cancer she just died from.

She thrashed her head away from Andrew to see Dr. Harlow right there. She blasted a deadly stare back at Andrew. "You can't kill what's already dead." She looked away from him, shocked that her voice worked and those words came out. She tried desperately to get away.

"You're not dead, dear. You're purified," Dr. Harlow said.

She felt a prick from a needle.

"Bring in Mason, to meet Linda," Dr. Harlow continued.

***

The door blew open as Andrew flew out with Steve behind him. Andrew was not sure which way to go, and his initial search of the area showed nothing unusual. He took off without Steve, searching urgently.

Andrew rounded a corner. He saw Mason squirming on the ground between the two buildings. He ran there, unfolding a straitjacket. Andrew turned to see Steve coming up from behind him, fumbling for something in his pocket.

Andrew jumped on Mason, but Mason didn't react. He only fought with his own head. Steve jumped in and secured him while Andrew worked his arm into the jacket. Mason began to struggle.

With the second arm secure, Steve stepped away letting Andrew finish the job. He pulled both Mason's arms in tight and hauled him up so they were face to face. After a smile of superiority, he spun Mason around, and began to buckle up the straps like he was a master at this.

Andrew pulled extra tight on the last strap, intending to make sure Mason knew who he was dealing with. He put his foot into Mason's back, kicked him away, and stepped beside Steve. The alarm still blasted from inside the building. He watched Mason fight the jacket and thrash his head. Mason turned violently to him, but Andrew wasn't the least bit concerned. He let him suffer a while longer, then took a remote from Steve. He pushed a button. The alarm stopped, and Mason collapsed to the ground.

CHAPTER 36

Mason was pushed into the small building and past the hallway he fled down during his escape. He had never been where he was heading, but he knew nothing good would come from it. Before he had time to react, his feet flew out from under him. His journey began; the stairs were first. The straitjacket did nothing to protect him as he tumbled down. He came to a crashing stop against Dr. Harlow.

"Not so fast, Mason."

Mason could see his face inches away. He felt Dr. Harlow grab him, so Mason curled up to protect himself.

"I'm sorry, but I have nothing to offer you."

Mason looked at him. Dr. Harlow was genuinely concerned.

"Andrew, cookies or possibly cakes?"

Mason barely knew which way was up, but he was

conscious and working on finding his feet. He felt Dr. Harlow grab the jacket again. At first the pull was weak, but suddenly Mason was upright. He was turned around, and Andrew was in control.

"Mason, come, come," Dr. Harlow said with childlike excitement. "You'll love this. I know it."

Mason made an attempt to get back up the stairs. Andrew threw him up against the wall. He fell to the ground like a wet rag. Mason cringed in pain. He rolled himself tight again but was hauled up and pushed through a door.

Being dragged down the hallway seemed like eternity to Mason. He tried to get on his feet, but Andrew's persistent aggression made that impossible. It finally ended with a toss into the supply room.

Mason fell into a shelf; medical supplies crashed. He slipped on them as he tried to stay upright, but pain got the best of him. He staggered into a table, nearly knocking over the capsule filling machine. The cup holding capsules hit the ground. Mason noticed they were the same as the single capsule Dr. Harlow gave him.

Mason suddenly realized all this violent activity would likely make him change again and if he did... He made an attempt to get the capsules, but Andrew quickly had him moving. He was thrown into the other hallway. Mason looked back, desperately knowing how much he needed those capsules.

He started to get up and saw Dr. Harlow farther ahead, heading into another room. He was pushed from behind by the unforgiving tyrant. The doorway was his only destination, but he was redirected into a support post, sticking out from the wall.

Mason staggered off it and fell through the doorway of the common room. He looked up and saw Dr. Harlow. Then he saw everyone else including Bob Robinson standing right in front of him.

Bob backed up.

"Bob, take him out!" Mason shouted. He looked at everyone else. "All of us, and they won't stand a chance." He was shocked that all they did was watch.

Bob turned away.

"What?" Mason squirmed frantically trying to get to him.

Bob turned back and continued watching Mason with the others but still did nothing to help.

"Bob, trust me. This is your only chance," Mason pleaded.

Bob kept his distance.

Mason looked at him curiously. "Whose damn side are you on?" Suddenly, Mason was on his feet again. "Don't tell me—" He was slammed against the wall.

"Discoveries, discoveries. Nothing but discoveries around here," Andrew said.

"I have someone just for you, Mason," Dr. Harlow proudly said.

Mason was being forced toward the door. "For me?" He pointed to everyone else in the room but barely could because of Andrew's aggressiveness. "Who are they for? And those, those freaks out there. What's that—"

"My mistakes? But you're better than them, Mason." Dr. Harlow reached out to touch him as Mason almost fell. "You and now—" Dr. Harlow opened the door and disappeared behind it.

"But all I ever wanted was my life back. Why couldn't you just give me that?" Mason yelled, pleading to the doctor who was no longer there.

Again, Mason was pushed through the doorway. He saw Jill watching from the other side of the room. He made an attempt to go to her but was held back.

"You can watch, but you can't touch," Andrew whispered arrogantly.

"Because you're much more than that. The Mason I created has nothing to do with that Mason," Dr. Harlow said.

Mason watched him checking on someone—a woman, wired up and laying in a bed. She was awake but heavily sedated.

Dr. Harlow turned back. "That Mason is dead."

Mason was pushed again, but he gave no resistance. It left him sprawled out on the floor, wrapped up tight in the straitjacket. Dr. Harlow was there instantly. He caressed Mason's bald head then held his face in his hands like a father would his dying son.

"You've been there," Dr. Harlow said. "This Mason has completed the final stage."

Mason felt tugging on the straps behind his back.

"This Mason's magnificent. This Mason is miraculous. This Mason has evolved."

The tugging stopped, and Mason's head was pulled up.

"And she's just like you."

Mason looked at the woman in the bed. He looked back to Dr. Harlow who suddenly let him go like a little girl dropping her baby doll would. Mason watched him go to the woman. He looked back to Mason, suddenly very confused.

Then he swung his attention over to another patient—a man, still unconscious. "But so is he." He rushed to him. He rubbed his forehead with the same passion he just had for Mason.

Mason watched the woman who looked desperately at him through her drug hazed eyes. To Mason, she was alive and the closest person here he could relate to. By the way she looked at him, she felt the same.

Dr. Harlow turned quickly, catching Mason's attention. He stared a death sentence at Mason. The compassion suddenly disappeared. "I don't like you anymore." He paused, seeming unsure of himself. He looked to the woman then back to the man. "I don't trust you anymore," he said reluctantly. He started breathing heavily, but it only came out as panting. He attempted to whistle but ended up blowing spit.

Then Mason watched his expression completely change. Anger took over. He began to snort with each heavy breath. He pulled violently at the man's covers. He snapped back to Mason with confidence. "I don't want you anymore, Mason. You've betrayed me, and I don't need you."

He bolted away from the beds and went directly to Jill,

grabbing a scalpel from a table he passed. "I don't need her to get you back either." He flung himself at her and started hacking at the duct tape that bound her wrists. "You can have her, Mason," he yelled.

Jill forced out a muffled scream as blood poured. She struggled to get away, but Dr. Harlow kept hacking.

Mason knew he was oblivious to what he was doing. Mason tried to get to her, but he was held down.

Dr. Harlow started sobbing. "My first has grown up, and now he wants to leave. Little does he care about all that was his. Little does he care about those who care about him. He has his own life now…"

Mason watched helplessly as he hacked deeper.

"And with that life, he will leave me forever." Dr. Harlow's head sunk with his final slashes at Jill's wrists. He pushed her away like she was free to go.

Mason knew Jill wasn't going anywhere. Blood poured from both her wrists leaving her lifeless. Dr. Harlow's push just made her fall over as she continued to bleed out.

Dr. Harlow didn't even notice. Suddenly, he was completely rejuvenated as though he himself was born again. "Andrew!" He screamed and bolted, past Andrew, for the door.

Mason struggled to his feet and made another attempt to get to Jill. He was slammed back down, flat on his back. He tried again but Andrew had him moving for the door. With a hefty push through it, Mason was back to being led by Dr. Harlow's strong arm.

CHAPTER 37

Mason knew the room as soon as he was tossed into it. Although he was about to crash violently again, he intentionally directed his fall toward the table with the capsules underneath it. It was too small in here for any second chances, so Mason knew he had to make this work. It would look to Andrew as though he was trying to hide, but Mason knew exactly what he wanted. The capsules had been here only minutes ago. Unless someone was on janitor duty during Mason's aggressive unwelcoming, there was no reason why they still wouldn't be.

Mason's eyes closed from the impact of his fall when Andrew's iron claws clamped down on him again. Mason shot open his eyes. He grabbed at nothing, desperately trying to focus, but instantly he was off for another body toss.

Going up the stairs was a lot less painful than going down,

but the pavement outside was merciless. Mason had nothing left when he was pulled up and led to the blue van.

If it wasn't for the flight of stairs at the beginning of all this, I'd have this bastard at the other end of the stick. Meet me in a bar after midnight. He shook his head trying to clear the daze. He saw the field he escaped into. If he could only get a chance to run through it again. This time he wouldn't go back to Rocksbrough; not to his friends—they didn't need his shit; not to Jill—she'd already forgotten about him. *Just another chance—my God, Jill…* He turned back to the door, but he could only look.

Mason was thrown up against the van which broke his daydream. He shook his head to clear his mind and hopefully the pain. "You already got your chance," he quietly said to himself. "Everyone else would have just died."

The van door slid open, and Mason shot Andrew a stare of revenge as he was thrown inside. Andrew just smiled back with a snorting chuckle.

***

Mason bounced on the floor of the van as it moved fast, jolted forward, and veered sharply. A stretcher shook violently beside him. Although it wasn't very comfortable back here, he was no longer being mauled by a human pit bull. He still wore the straitjacket, but no one had taken the time to buckle up the belts Dr. Harlow loosened. He worked to free his arms.

A sharp corner sent him flying into the stretcher, breaking it from its supports. It bounced uncontrollably. The stretcher's leg came down on his arm. Mason screamed in agony and a sealed capsule, clenched tight in his fist, fell free. He grabbed his arm and looked frantically for the capsule. At the same time, he felt his body start to change.

Mason grasped on to the stretcher as his back began to ripple. His eyes searched for the capsule, but he abandoned that to deal with this imminent transition. He took cover under the stretcher to conceal himself from Andrew. He rolled up tight and tried to stay calm.

Quickly, all the pain stopped. There was no more suffering. All he had endured was over, and now Andrew would have to deal with a new Mason—a Mason Andrew had no chance against.

Mason grunted, almost like a growl, as the van grinded to a sudden stop. Everything in the back shifted forward including Mason. He smashed against the seats, but pain was no longer an issue. He came within inches of Andrew, but Andrew never looked back.

The driver's door slammed shut and a sudden silence remained for Mason to enjoy. He looked around the van and at himself. He felt a sense of ownership with this new body. Something he felt comfortable with—at peace with—but it didn't last long.

Both back doors opened. Andrew stood in the opening holding a gun at his side. He was a target impossible to miss, and the unaimed gun didn't offer him any protection. Mason grabbed on to the stretcher and hurled it at Andrew. A direct hit cleared him away. The stretcher bounced to a crashing halt outside, and Andrew squirmed on the ground from the impact. Mason saw the gun lying beside him.

He launched himself at Andrew with two knees flying into his shoulders. Mason strangely planted two feet in the ground above Andrew's head. With his knees pinning Andrew, he buried his elbow into Andrew's face.

"You, son of a bitch. You've used your last corpse," Mason growled.

He rolled off while wrapping a long sleeve from the straitjacket around Andrew's neck. He pulled tight then used the jacket to haul him onto his feet.

"Purify gave me back a life I can't live."

Andrew's eyes bulged from choking. He tried desperately to free the sleeve, but his efforts were just hands grabbing at nothing.

"I'm a criminal, a fugitive..." Mason relieved the pressure and released him.

Andrew gasped for air then struggled with a raspy response. "A freak."

Mason smashed him up against the open van door. He was inches from Andrew, but he saw his own face in the reflection from the window. He pushed himself away. He held his head as he spun around, torn with grief. Four legs controlled his movement. Two hands ripped the jacket away freeing the other two—clawed and supporting webs. He stood there, directly in front of Andrew, postured as this new human. He looked to the sky and stretched his arms up as far as he could.

"I've done nothing wrong!" Mason yelled.

Suddenly, he lunged toward Andrew and ripped the other door off. He crushed it like corrugated cardboard.

"I beat up a guy for taking everything I've worked for." Mason screamed as he hurled the door into the van.

"I didn't even know that doctor."

Mason spun around, back to Andrew. He was just breathing now—heavy, with panting cries. He looked to the ground; to the gun.

"And I never killed Reg," he said calmly. He looked up to Andrew.

Mason took a step toward him. "Death, was my only mistake."

He took another step then he surged with his hand wide open. He grabbed on to Andrew's face and paused with the feeling of having full control. Then he slammed Andrew's head back with extreme force causing it to splash against the window.

Mason felt Andrew instantly become lifeless. The back of his head was cracked open with its contents oozing out. His face slid out of Mason's hand, and he fell into a heap on the ground.

Mason stepped back and looked at his attacker. He looked at his hand, then the bloodstained window. He was relatively calm and fell into a trance. Andrew's lifeless body trembled on the ground in front of him. He knew what he had just done. It was more than he could have ever done in the past. He knew he was different now; he was different from anyone else. From this point on, this is what he would be capable of. But he wasn't ready for that.

Then he snapped out of it. He leaped into the back of the van, smashing everything in pursuit of the sealed capsule.

PART III

EXPOSED

CHAPTER 38

"Okay, I'm glad they're quiet... Thanks, mom... Talk to you in the morning." Stace hung up and put the phone down.

Normally, at this time of night, Stace would be going to great lengths to keep the house quiet. The daunting task of getting the kids to sleep, justified her insistence on keeping the television down and any movements soft.

This had never gone over well with Reg who hadn't been the type of guy who liked to tiptoe in the living room. If he'd been watching a game, well, Reg never just watched a game; so he would just change the channel. If he had wanted to eat, to avoid the unnecessary banging of cupboards and crashing of dishes, Stace would have stepped in right away and gotten something for him.

This night was different though. No kids were here to keep asleep, and there was no Reg at all. Just Stace, alone at the kitchen table with a phone.

A magazine was open, but she wasn't reading it. She just stared at it and her coffee. It was like she had just said something to both of them and waited for their reply. But no one, or nothing, was talking in Stace's house tonight. She had the quiet she always wanted, but now she couldn't help but wish for the next goal to score, the shocking clang of beer bottles, something to be thrown into the sink, Emma to start crying, and Kyle to peek his head around the corner and say, *I can't sleep, Mommy.* That's when Reg would put the television on mute, tiptoe to Kyle with his finger to his mouth, pick him up with a guilty smile for Stace, and head down the hall to fix what he just broke.

Stace sighed and sniffed. She wiped her eye before a tear was able to spill over and escape onto her cheek like so many before it. She had never been the crying type, but losing Reg and not knowing where the hell Mason was, had put her over the top. Now, all she could do was cry.

With the reality of Reg being gone, she had tried to focus her efforts on helping Mason. She had told Warren that Mason wasn't a murderer. She had insisted in fact, but all indicators pointed to Mason as Reg's killer. Now that he bolted, there wasn't a judge alive who would give her testimony as a character witness any consideration, even coming from the victim's wife.

That got her thinking about how ridiculous Mason's story really was. But she honestly believed him. This made her wonder what she would say to Reg if he walked through the door just like Mason had done for Jill. Everyone in her situation would want that to happen. Everyone except... She shook her head at the thought of Jill's reaction.

Suddenly, a crash came from the backyard. It stunned her, shattering the quietness. Stace was not the type who would react to a noise at night, even if she was alone. This time, for some unknown reason, she grabbed the phone and went to the kitchen window. There was nothing on the driveway and nothing toward the back. She gave a quick look to the front—again, nothing.

She turned away from the window and put the phone down. The magazine was on the table, but she decided she'd had enough of the front cover. She walked into the living room but went to the window instead of sitting down. From the center blinds, she just peeked out. She was still concerned about the noise although she would never admit it, even to herself.

***

Warren watched Stace's house from his unmarked car parked down the street. He wasn't concerned that Stace had just come to the window. That's just what people did to check things out for no apparent reason. He knew she was there; he knew the kids weren't. He didn't know if she had any way to get in touch with Mason though, so maybe the window check did mean something.

Mason was the only reason Warren was there at all.

Staking himself out in front of her house seemed like the right thing to do for a detective. His supervisor wanted more manpower doing surveillance on this sympathetic widow, but Warren insisted he would be the only one. Even though detectives routinely spy on others, he felt particularly creepy considering the woman at the window just lost her husband; and he recently lost his wife. Regardless of whether or not it was a good idea, he watched her, but she didn't linger. That left Warren looking at her closed blind.

***

Still unwilling to admit to herself that she was concerned about the noise, Stace stepped away from the window and looked down the hallway. *Just go look out the bedroom window. Prove I'm not officially over the edge.* She headed for the hallway.

From the window, she saw a lawn chair overturned on the patio. That was nothing. Except, it would have made the exact same sound. She looked closer at the patio then the whole backyard. She saw the shadow of a man on the driveway.

She snapped back.

A knock at the back door startled her more. She considered going there but returned quickly to the front window. She looked out from the side blinds this time and saw the rear end of a van under a street light, parked around the corner. It meant nothing to her specifically, but it did remind her of Kyle and the van. This added to the paranoid state she was already in. Also, the fact it was missing a door didn't help.

Then another, louder knock. She looked back. Now at least she knew she wasn't crazy, but she still considered it because she was scared shitless. *Jesus Christ, girl, settle down. Someone's knocking at the door. Big deal.* Her big girl talk didn't do much good though. She couldn't help notice her hand shaking as she slowly turned away from the window.

She entered the kitchen and started to walk through, toward the back door. She hesitated and stopped to lean against the table. While staring at the stove, she considered her next move. Instead of continuing to the back door, she went to the drawer below the oven.

***

Warren had given up on watching blinds, and he also had enough of observing dark driveways. Maybe Stace could use some company. He certainly could.

He stepped out of his car and walked across the road toward the house.

***

Mason moved slowly along the driveway from the back of the house. He saw Warren—exactly who he worried about. He quickly stepped back behind the house. He looked around frantically. What if the place was surrounded? Mason came here from the backyard, so he knew he needed to get back there. He dashed into the darkness.

***

Warren approached the house cautiously, not sure if this social visit would be the right technique with Stace. After all, every time they had met so far, she had always been against him. Even when he had tried to assure her they would stop at nothing to find Mason, she had gone on the defensive and taken Mason's side. But who knew, in a quiet moment, he may hit the right note and get her working with him.

Before knocking, he tried to see inside the house from the front door. He saw nothing, so he knocked. Nothing moved. He tried again. He waited with a cautious eye but nothing aroused it. He walked down the steps toward the driveway.

***

Stace stood in the dark at the back door. She slowly put her hand on the handle but hesitated turning it.

A knock scared the shit out of her.

She jumped back and forced her hand over her mouth. The screen door opened. Hidden in the darkness, she held her ground. Then the wooden door opened a crack. She braced herself. The door opened wide.

She swung—smash. A frying pan nailed Warren right on the forehead. He staggered back and crashed against the screen door. He hit the patio like a six foot piece of falling lumber.

Stace stood over him, shocked by her mistake. Then, another noise.

She looked up to see Mason standing in the backyard. The frying pan clanged against the patio stones while Stace backed up. She stopped with her back against the wall and Warren out cold in front of her.

While holding her chest, she said, "This heart can't take anymore." She started to cry.

Mason ran to her. "I'm so sorry, Stace." She held him tight. She noticed a tear running down Mason's cheek. Stace moved away and wiped her eyes. "It's not worth it, Mason." She touched his head, concerned that he was now bald. She noticed blood on the shirt he was wearing.

"If only I had a choice." He looked at Warren then back to her. "I didn't do it, Stace. You know I didn't do it, don't you?"

Stace said, "Of course." She looked at him while shaking her head. "You look so different." She looked away. "Everything's so different."

Mason didn't move. "You have no idea, Stace."

"I liked it better when you called me Skillet." She looked back and smiled. She picked up the frying pan.

She watched Mason staring at Warren, still out cold. He started to move away. "I can't stay here. I just finished telling myself that if I got another chance, I wouldn't come back. You don't need my shit." He stopped and turned back to her.

"But for some reason, I can't let go of what I had before."

"Leaving won't change that. It will just put it farther away—make things more difficult because you never solved anything."

"Farther away is where I need to be, to get away from him."

"Which makes you guiltier, in his eyes."

"How much guiltier can I be?"

"Much, if you actually did the things he thinks you did. But since you didn't, prove it. Prove your story, and the past will set you free."

"It's supposed to be the truth."

"You're telling the truth, so all you've got to prove is the past."

"And you believe all of this?"

"Yeah, I do. I also believe you keep coming back because this is where you belong. Not from way back when, but from this point on."

She dropped the frying pan. She stepped toward Mason.

"Don't leave, Mason. You can't leave me. I need you," Stace said urgently. She looked down and started to cry again. "What about the kids? Kyle doesn't have a dad to teach him how to play baseball, how to catch a fish, how to treat a girl. I need you here, not dead like Reg."

Mason shook his head stepping back. "Jill used me for everything I had." He looked away. "An insane doctor used me when I was supposed to be dead." He turned back to her. "And now you, to replace Reg."

Stace stormed him, pounding with both fists. "You bastard." He held her back. "There's a big difference between being used and needed." He let her go.

"Sure you need me, but do you love me?" Mason said.

She turned away holding her face. She looked back desperately.

"Do you love me?" Mason said again.

"Do you love me, Mason?"

He started to walk away. "I don't know what love is."

"Well I do!" she yelled. "And I know I've always loved you," she said softly.

He stopped.

"More than I ever loved Reg."

He turned back to her. "Do you even know who I am?"

"You're Mason Bushing."

"You can't dig me up for proof."

"Don't need to. You're standing right in front of me."

The screen door squeaked. She turned to it; Warren moved.

CHAPTER 39

Mason couldn't believe that he and Stace actually helped Warren onto a chair at the kitchen table. He figured he should be getting away from him or doing whatever he could to keep him down. He had his chance to run, but he didn't. He had his chance to pound on this mouthpiece, whose arm was now draped over his shoulder, but he didn't do that either. Having this annoying detective around was the last thing he needed while he tried to straighten things out with Stace. Surely they could have done something else like tie him up or just leave him outside in a heap on the patio slabs.

But Stace's words about solving it made him realize this would be the only way to get past everything, and Warren was the guy he would have to convince. So there Mason was, nursing the big lug who never gave a shit about him, even when he hurt way more than this friggin' nosy cop's headache must have.

Since Mason had always been at Warren's mercy, he felt pretty good about finally having the upper hand. That made him want to take a few shots just for the sake of getting even, but if he stayed cool, he should get one last chance to sell his story. Right here; right now. It was just a matter of how he presented it. He remembered though, this was Warren the Detective he was dealing with. Not only did he have a head of cement, but it all dried up on Mason's case a while back. Convincing him would fall just short of a miracle, but he thought he might as well try because he was different now. Without any of those capsules, it was just a matter of time before Mason was on his own without ever being able to look back.

"I should have hit him with the pan again, myself. At least that way I could do some talking for a change," Mason said to Stace. *Even though I haven't got a clue what I'm going to say to this moron.*

Warren sat, holding his head in his hands. "Well, choose the right words because this is the only chance you've got before both of you are talkin' downtown."

"Still a tough guy, and you can't even walk."

"Oh, I'm not worried. I'll walk again soon, but not you."

Mason took a chair across the table from him. He looked hard at Warren. "I've gone this far, and you still think I'm scammin'?"

"What's so hard to understand? Your story sucks."

"Were you always an asshole? Wouldn't I just disappear?"

"I believe it. Reg didn't, but I do," Stace said.

Mason looked at her leaning against the counter.

"Well you're the only one, sweetheart," Warren said.

She continued. "That old man with Kyle at the van... He ran over me in the pathway. I told you that before. Something's not right there."

Warren nodded, confirming his understanding. "That and your wife are the only reasons you're here."

No, the reason I'm here and not in your damn cage, is because you got cocky, again, which gave me a chance to run; and you haven't seen me since, you fuckin' tuna. Mason leaned into the table. "You didn't think I should know that? Do you think I might not have run if you'd told me that?" He shook his head in disbelief. "What's stoppin' me from ending your God damn badge balls right now?"

Warren reached for his gun. He banged it down on the table. "There's your shot."

Mason held his ground with tension as thick as the animosity between them. He didn't make a move, but he showed no weakness either.

Warren rubbed the sore spot on his forehead, obviously not interested in making it any worse. "There's something about Jill I don't understand. She wants the money more than you. I never got that."

Mason kept his stone face, but that wasn't the way he was thinking. *He just put a loaded gun right in front of a desperate man. My God, he trusts me. But does he believe me?*

Warren picked up the gun. He put it back in its holster.

Mason saw his badge case fall on the floor.

Warren turned to Stace. "You've already got what I'd do anything to get. Do you think Harlow makes deliveries?"

Mason said, "So you finally believe me?"

Warren chuckled. "No, Mason, I'm a lot smarter than that. It's the pain in my head that makes me say stupid things." Warren bent over to pick up his badge. He winced in pain. "So what's your plan now, Mason? And please, no more dead guys or frying pans."

I don't have a friggin' plan.

Stace picked the case up with a picture showing.

"Shit's stackin' up so high in front of you, tell me you're not gonna try runnin' right through it."

Stace handed it to Warren, but he was preoccupied with the pain. She put it on the table.

The picture faced Mason.

"Focus on something else," Warren said. He went to take the badge, but Mason grabbed his arm with his eyes on the picture. He leaned in for a closer look.

"What?" Warren said.

Mason said nothing. He continued staring at the picture.

"Do you even know who she is?" Warren continued.

Mason stood up and walked around the table. *Do I even know who she is?* Mason thought it couldn't possibly be her. Just because she had blonde hair, the same as the woman in the picture. Just because the woman in the picture looked just like her—at least he thought they looked the same. It hadn't been that long ago; he hardly saw her at all. She was lifeless, but yeah, they do look the same. But it couldn't possibly be the same woman Dr. Harlow was so anxious to show him. *My God...* Now he knew why Dr. Harlow was all over himself. *He was building the future, and we were the beginning. But the woman in Warren's picture?* If it was her, then this thing was a done deal. That's assuming, of course, he could get Warren to believe she was in the Purify program. He certainly wouldn't take Mason's word for it. Other than that, what the hell else could he do to convince him? But if it wasn't... *Yeah, so, big deal if it's not her.* He'd be no worse off than he was now. The only difference was that Warren would go over the top and heads would roll. *Bottom line is, now I've got a plan, and I better make it work.*

Stace was suddenly in front of him. She stopped him from pacing. "Mason? You look like you're gonna puke or something."

Mason snapped out of it. He looked to Warren, but the picture was gone.

Warren patted his pocket. "She's my wife. Unlike you, if I dig her up, she'll be there."

"What makes you so sure?" Mason looked at Stace then the window. He turned back to Warren.

"You said you'd do anything to get her back. Let's see if the doctor's in."

Mason noticed Stace curiously watching him. He saw Warren look at her with a squinched up face. "He wants me to visit the magnificent miracle medic. Can we assume he's officially taken the plunge?" He looked at Mason. "We can call someone."

"You need proof?" Mason said.

"Proof about what?"

Mason tapped Warren's pocket.

"Why do you care about Linda?" Warren said slowly tilting his head like he was catching on.

Did he say Linda? Mason remembered Dr. Harlow calling her Linda. He closed his eyes and gulped. He turned away and saw Stace looking out the window. She looked back to him. He nodded slowly.

"Then I'll give you proof by the shovel full". Mason turned to Stace. "We can do it tonight."

Warren sat forward in his chair. "Do it tonight... Do what, tonight?"

Mason watched Stace look out the window again then she left the room, heading for the backdoor.

"Why Linda, Mason?"

Mason didn't respond. He could hear the door open and close.

"Mason, answer me."

There was the sound of metal banging outside. Something was thrown into a truck bed.

"Mason—"

Mason looked out the window. He saw Reg's truck. He stared back at Warren. "Because where she is…" He looked away. "Is a lie, according to you."

Warren jumped up from his chair. "Bullshit you son of a bitch." Warren grabbed his head from the sudden blood rush.

"Catch me off guard and vulnerable. Now you try to suck me into your Purify scam. Come on, Mason. You must have something better than this."

"Where did she die, Warren? Rocksbrough Memorial Hospital just like me, right?"

Warren looked away holding his head.

"Where was she prepared? Was it Rocksbrough Funeral Home?"

Warren spun around and looked Mason straight in the eye. He suddenly lost all his cockiness. He was obviously the confused one now.

"I thought so. How much is anything, Warren?" Mason heard the truck start. "Where did you bury Linda?"

Warren ran for the door as though he would plow right through it. Mason watched him pull it open and burst outside.

Mason stepped outside. Warren was at the driver's door.

"You don't really think I'm gonna stand here and let you guys dig up my wife do you?" Warren shouted at Stace.

"It's what we're all looking for, Warren. But you're right, no one's going anywhere without you showing us where," Stace said.

Stace looked at Mason then back to Warren. "I watched that man dying then I buried him. Now he's right here. We both know it's him, but how did that happen, Warren?"

Warren didn't respond.

Mason passed him and went directly to the passenger door. "I know where your life is," he said with the confidence

Warren lacked.

CHAPTER 40

Mason sat in the truck watching Warren's car up ahead. There was no conversation between him and Stace. He couldn't remember a time when words were not found to express how they felt. But now was different. Words were said that probably never should have been. Of course, that was only because Reg was dead which somehow made their affair worse to Mason. Other than rattles an old truck makes and road noise from truck tires, it was as quiet in here as the country road they drove along.

Because he would soon discover what Dr. Harlow was burying, Mason started thinking if he could remember any part of Dr. Harlow taking him after he died. He remembered clearly his death; even his last breath. No one had been with him except a single nurse. She was nice, comforting, and the only one to see him die. He remembered preferring it that way, rather than everyone standing over him like he was giving them an intimate performance of his passing. He hadn't fought the final gasps for air. Instead, he had worked them like a strip set of cross body curls. They were relieving after all the suffering he had gone through with cancer. Along with a sudden feeling of warmth rushing through his body, they gave him strength despite what was about to happen. It had all come down to those last breaths which turned into his basic representation of the life he was about to lose.

But after the last breath, he didn't remember anything. He thought hard, but he came up with nothing. The next thing that happened was the first time he met Dr. Harlow. He remembered thinking strange things about guardian angels and St. Peter, but there were no gates to pass through. No one with long hair and flowing robes had been there to greet him. He wasn't in the same place he last remembered, but he definitely wasn't in the skies above or six feet below.

Now Mason would find out what Dr. Harlow did to cover for the missing corpses he routinely stole. How many empty caskets lay in the cemeteries around here? How many people go to these sites and pay their respects to nothing? How many Warren's were out there who still have this to deal with when the whole thing is exposed? He turned his attention away from the car and looked out the side window at darkness. *How many Jill's will there be?*

"He could be the liar you know—settin' you up or something," Stace said, breaking the silence.

Mason looked back to Warren's car. "How would that go

down? You don't sound convinced yourself." He gave Stace a curious look. *Fuck me. Don't tell me you're bailin'.* The last thing Mason needed was to lose the loyalty of Stace. But if he really thought about it, she probably was wondering what the fuck she was doing here. This wasn't her fight, and she had so much to risk being part of it. Maybe she was just now realizing that. Maybe she would drop the bomb and leave him to figure this out with Warren. Mason sighed with the thought of that. He nodded to himself because that clearly made sense. "Listen, Stace, don't put yourself through what's not your problem."

"What makes you think it's not my problem?" she quickly said.

"Even if you think it is—the kids, they're your problem."

She didn't reply.

Mason realized he was wrong. She wasn't thinking of abandoning him. He was the one who just put that bug in her ear. But that was okay. Clearly, she shouldn't be here. But there was no doubt about it, he didn't want her to leave.

The truck went quiet again. Stace's mind was obviously turning up a storm. She stared straight ahead then looked to Mason. She started to talk but stopped. She stared ahead again.

Mason wanted to say something, but he wasn't sure what. *Shit. Just Warren and me? Who knows how that will turn out?*

"No. I'm here and I'm going to see it through," she said without turning her attention off the road. She nodded. "Just the type of girl I am, I guess."

Mason smiled. "Just the type of girl I'm looking for." He looked at her. The quiet drive continued, but the awkward tension was gone. Mason cleared his throat with a gulp to hold down the lump. "I saw his wife there, but if this doesn't work…"

She looked at him. "You went back?"

Mason nodded. "And left behind a trail of madness." He looked out the side window.

"Jill's there too."

The car suddenly swerved. Stace controlled it.

"Was there…" But where is she now? He knew what Dr. Harlow did with his rejects which, in some obscure respect, was at least humane. But what about the ones that hadn't made it? Did he throw them in the field out there, or were they littered throughout the district and left for guys like Warren to deal with? He shook his head and continued to watch the road.

He saw a sign: "*Lordstown.*"

CHAPTER 41

Mason stepped out from the truck and looked across the road at Lordstown's cemetery. It was just like any other small town cemetery, and the night sky left it dark just like any other night. Mason thought about cemeteries and nighttime not mixing well together, especially if excavation activities were planned. But if there was going to be unwanted digging here, this was the time to do it. Since Mason would be the one holding the shovel, he felt security from the darkness. He was even more comfortable knowing he had a cop watching out.

Mason took a shovel and an edger from the truck. He looked back to see Warren's car parked inconspicuously, further down the road. The headlights were off, but Mason knew he was there. The last time they talked, or had any kind of communication, was in the driveway at Stace's place. There were no cell phones for texting or making calls. They used no hand gestures or sign language of any kind. They simply followed him. The fact that Warren led them here told Mason he was okay with what was about to happen, but Warren wasn't moving which made it obvious he wanted nothing to do with it. Mason was fine with that. He really only needed Warren for one thing—to confirm nothing was there when the lid opened.

Mason leaned the tools against the truck then knelt down. He took the gun Andrew had dropped and moved it under the waist of his pants—Andrew's pants. Before getting up, he looked across the road at the cemetery. For some reason it seemed more normal to Mason if he had a body to put into the ground, rather than digging to find one already there. The fact that he was looking for something that shouldn't be here didn't make this any better, but it did feel less criminal to him. *I wonder if that's how a judge will see it.* He stood up tall, took the shovels, and began his walk to fate.

***

Mason walked slowly with a flashlight, looking closely at headstones. Stace was with him, but she didn't do much searching. He noticed she was on edge about something, but finding a rock in a field wasn't it.

He searched from headstone to headstone then realized that finding the right one could take longer than digging. He didn't have a watch to know what time it was, but time would never be on his side for something like this. He continued to the next marker, quickly skimming over it. He moved on then realized he didn't really read the last one. He went back to it. He looked closer. The headstone read: *"Linda Rosemary Fillmore, Always Loved and Never Forgotten, 1979 - 2013."*

***

As Mason stood over the grave site with the shovel in his hand, he hesitated putting the blade into the ground. He thought that instead of this being so ominous, it should be ceremonious—marking the rediscovery of lives thought lost. He thought about being surrounded by all the Lordstown VIPs. Instead, he figured the Mayor was likely sound asleep. The Fire Chief was probably playing euchre with the rest of his crew. The Chief of Police would definitely be busy staked out in front of the town's drinking hole after last call, and the Coroner, who would have authorized any exhumation, probably didn't even know where Lordstown was. The most important thing to Mason was that none of these guys were anywhere near this place. Any dreams of being a hero would have to wait until all the dirty work was done and all the ghosts were exposed.

After he threw the first shovel of dirt, Mason lost all thought of sudden fame. The task at hand took over. He dug aggressively while Stace started to carefully work on an outline with the edger. He took note of the pile of dirt they created which helped hide the fact active digging was in process. Motivated by the fear of getting caught and the end result, Mason was surprised how easy it was to move each shovel of earth he carved into.

He stopped and took a second to examine their progress. He wiped his forehead and watched Stace continue. Mason looked over to the road to check that Warren still provided cover. Satisfied, he started up again then stopped. He heard a car and faint music.

The music got louder and suddenly gravel flew when a car fishtailed into the cemetery. Headlights briefly flashed Mason. The car stopped. Music blared but no one moved—from the car or the hole. Both Mason and Stace watched the car, but there was still no movement from it. Then a scream, combined with a girlish laugh, overpowered the music.

Mason jumped out of the hole and rolled down the mound of dirt. He peered over the mound like he was on the front line in the battle of Lordstown.

The passenger door swung open. A girl ran out. "On our first date, you take me to a cemetery?" she said.

She headed straight toward Mason. She must have noticed the mound of dirt because she stopped.

Mason ducked down as if the first shot had been taken. He checked to see if Stace was still there. She was down as low as she could get. Their eyes met and the message between them said nothing but fear.

Mason slowly looked again to see a guy catch the girl.

"Come on, Susie." He turned her toward him.

"No way, Nick. We're in a damn cemetery."

He teased her back toward the car. "So. If you're scared,

that's what I'm here for."

Mason breathed a sigh of relief that the enemy was distracted. But how long would it last, he wondered?

"I said no! Not here," Susie shouted and tried to get away.

Mason saw Stace sneak over to the side of the dirt pile and look to the road. She pulled herself back to Mason.

"I said no!" Mason heard Susie yell. "You're not gettin' laid in a cemetery."

He saw another car enter the driveway. A blue light started flashing from the front window. Mason watched Susie run back to their car and Nick slowly follow.

Warren got out. He carried a flashlight and showed Nick his badge. They talked for a second then Warren tapped him lightly on the shoulder. Nick headed for his car.

It started with a roar. Loud music blared again; a rev of the engine, and it spun away.

Warren looked around at first. He turned to his car but didn't go. He quickly walked straight to the hole.

Mason stayed behind the dirt, making sure no other surprises popped up behind Warren. Satisfied, Mason stood up.

Warren looked in the hole. He shone the light on the headstone. He took a second to read what he had inscribed on it. "How much longer?"

Mason jumped back into the hole. He started digging. "What time is it?"

"Just after three."

Stace appeared with her edger.

Mason said, "I've got to get down at least three feet and clean the sides so the lid will open."

Mason looked up from digging when Warren took the edger from Stace.

"Move over."

"We've got it. This is the pile of shit you were talking about, and I doubt you want to be the one who runs through it," Mason said.

"Means nothin' if she's not here." Warren jumped in. Mason moved slightly as Warren started to dig.

"Do you know how to open this thing?"

Warren didn't look up. "Can't be any more difficult than the can of worms you've already cracked, right?"

Mason dug in the center giving room for Warren to work on the sides. Mason couldn't help realize what Warren just did. It was monumental in his fight for freedom. Maybe his testimony about Warren being a co-conspirator would be useless, but Stace was here. Since Warren knew that, it meant he was willing to go down this road. Mason understood why Warren stayed in the car. Denial was still in play at that point. But now, he seemed to have lost hope in his own justice system and was willing to put in whatever it took to get his wife back, all or nothing. Of course the nothing part would mean Linda was under here. If that was the case, Mason might as well join her and call it a day, or night. Of course with Warren here, that likely wouldn't be Mason's decision. Warren would be more than willing to give Mason the burial he never had.

Mason threw the blade in for another shovel full of dirt. He kicked the shovel deeper into the ground. There was a thud. Warren turned. Mason looked at Stace overhead.

Warren pushed the edger into the dirt beside where Mason was digging—another thud.

***

Mason cleared dirt from the sides of the hole while Warren worked with his hands around the casket latch. Mason moved to the corners, exposing the full lid. Warren fumbled with the latch and cleared more dirt. He twisted the mechanism and tried to lift the lid. It didn't move.

Mason removed more dirt. He watched Warren try again. The lid still didn't budge.

Mason worked to clear more dirt with Warren joining in. Warren tried again. The lid moved this time. Mason pulled himself out of the hole. He watched Warren pull harder and suddenly, air rushed in.

Mason looked straight down at his moment of truth. It actually reminded him of just before he died. The idea of leaving everything behind for what was about to happen made him feel like death was knocking again. He closed his eyes but only for a second.

Warren looked up at Mason. With his hands still on the lid, he pulled it up.

Death never looked so peaceful.

Mason watched Warren staring at the opened casket filled

with his decaying wife. Warren looked away and buried his head into his trembling hands.

Mason shook his head slowly and stared down at a corpse that represented the end of everything he had gone through. How could it possibly be? Had he wanted Dr. Harlow's victim to be the Linda in that picture too much? She had to be someone, but she wasn't Linda—not Warren's Linda. Now, it was a question of what to do. He looked away and quickly realized he was back where he started—another field to run through with no food, no money, no identity. But this time it wasn't the frail, old Dr. Harlow he had to deal with.

Suddenly, Warren jumped out of the hole and lunged. Mason hit the ground with Warren landing on top.

Mason protected himself, but the sudden movement of skin on his back took over. He started a heavy breathing routine while Warren began a brutal attack.

"You just told your last lie," Warren growled while he landed punch after punch. "And there's no doctor here to—"

Mason fired his arm into Warren's chest, sending him flying ten feet back. Mason tried to calm himself. His back rippled with movement.

Stace calmly said, "Did you bury your wife in a lab gown?"

Mason saw Warren's confusion. Warren rushed to the coffin. He took the left arm and looked at the hand.

Mason breathed heavily and concentrated on watching Warren.

Warren grabbed the flashlight from Stace. He looked closely at the corpse's hair. He looked to Stace. "It's not her."

Suddenly, a third arm rolled. It startled Warren—scared the shit out of him. He jumped out and started to run toward his car.

"Warren, hold on," Mason shouted. He felt quickly behind his back and the ripples were gone, but the gun wasn't.

Warren stopped. He looked back.

"We have to fill it back in," Mason said.

"Fuck that."

Mason didn't move. Stace stood beside him with the flashlight. "I can't go there," he said to her. He held on to the back of his head. He was confused and scared like a mouse who knew the cat was watching.

Warren stepped back to them. He squinted his eyes at Mason's sudden reluctance. "Hey, pal, you've got an audience now. Time for the encore don't you think?"

Stace shone the light on Mason's hand. Mason reluctantly gave in, revealing a scar on his skull.

"Harlow's a brain surgeon now?" Warren said.

"If I get too close…" Mason closed his eyes then looked back to the hole. "Shit, now what?" he said to himself.

"Don't you fuckin' dare take me this far then tell me we can't go."

"It's not as simple as just breaking in yelling 'Stop everything. I'm Warren the Detective.' He's got all of that covered. We won't get in unnoticed."

Warren grabbed Mason by the shoulders.

Mason broke free. "Just let me think about it." He turned

away.

Warren grabbed him again. He forced eye contact. "This part's simple—no thinking required. Where's my wife?"

CHAPTER 42

Mason had been at the back of the small building enough times to know they were in the right place, at least he thought they were. The abandoned basketball court, the other building, the field... It was all the same. He shook his head, confused, while looking at the door he escaped from. It was wide open.

He looked frantically around to see if anything else was different. Without giving it enough time to be truly sure, he rushed through the door and to the stairs where he stopped. He remembered what happened the last time he was here. He had the same urgency; the same fear. The only difference was he had time to contemplate what to do next. Reluctantly, he went down.

At the bottom, he looked up to see Warren and Stace. He was relieved his trip down went much better than last time, and that no one would put a ruthless spin on anything. He was only concerned about what he would show them. Everything Mason said rested on this building, and by the looks of it, what they were about to see wasn't going to match up.

He turned to the opened door and the hallway. He moved quickly into the supply room. It was stripped clean. The rollout trays were still here but empty. The table had nothing on it, but Mason had to see for himself if there were any capsules on the floor. He dove down and searched but came up with nothing. Overwhelmed, he came out from beneath the table to see Stace at the door and Warren searching like any detective would. Stace was obviously wondering what he was doing. Warren didn't seem to care though. Mason wondered if Warren had already given up on finding Linda and was now just resorting to his instinct of investigating. Mason took a second to think of something to say to Stace, but he decided nothing would be best. He went to the other door and reluctantly entered the hallway beyond it.

Mason entered the common room. It wasn't empty, but it was abandoned. The beds were here, and the television—everything was still in place that kept those in the program occupied. All that was missing were the patients which, of course, was the only thing Mason wanted to see. *And where the fuck are they? Shit.*

Ahead was the door to the procedure room. Mason already knew what he would see in there. He made a move toward the door but stopped when Warren and Stace came into the room. He realized that surprise must be the emotion he displayed, but really, disappointment consumed him. All the excitement he had built up inside, led him here thinking it would be all over. He shook his head realizing how naive he'd been. He missed the signs that should have told him this is what he would find. The fact that Dr. Harlow had already moved once. *Shit, I had even thought about Harlow running.* Of course, the biggest sign was that his head didn't go off. He touched the scar and headed toward the procedure room.

Inside, he looked around. Just a shell of the makeshift laboratory remained. The broken down, unused equipment was still here. The boxes, shelves, trays—all still making the room a mess. But there were no working monitors, no Linda, no other guy, and no Dr. Harlow.

"How far could they go?" Mason said really to himself. He looked at Stace. "With all that equipment, and a guy still in recovery?" He didn't expect an answer.

"What about Linda?" Warren impatiently said.

Mason moved to the beds. "Right here. I saw her, awake, in this bed." Mason shook his head. He remembered her looking at him. He remembered the instant relationship they had from just eye contact.

He saw Warren trying to take everything in. Mason looked around thinking about what his next move should be. He knew he had to come up with something, because Warren not only looked for evidence, he surely was still looking for his wife. *Without her, who knows where that will leave me?* He looked back to her bed but came up with nothing.

His eyes fell on the corner where he last saw Jill. The floor was still bloodstained which sent his mind spinning. He instantly remembered Dr. Harlow hacking at her wrists, and him not being able to do anything about it. He thought about Jill's obscure reaction at her front door when he came back. He remembered the last time he saw her before he died, then before that when they were happy together in their small house. He remembered looking forward to seeing her in the bar, and the first time they met; the love they had made which Mason had never been able to forget.

When the room came back into focus, he saw Warren kneeling down in front of the stain. He touched it, checking to see if it was still wet. He looked up to Mason. "Did you see this happen? It seems recent."

Mason said, "Yeah, I did."

Warren gave him a suspicious head tilt. "When would that have been, Mason?"

"I came back, but it didn't go well."

"Okay," Warren said, looking like a skeptic. "So what happened here? Someone was killed? There's enough blood…"

Mason was already nodding before Warren finished, but he could tell Warren wasn't buying it.

"Someone was killed… Someone you killed?" Warren's face showed nothing but confusion.

Mason didn't answer the question. He just stared down at the blood.

"Fuck me, Mason. There's a lot to process down here." Warren looked around the room again. "I'm not sure where—"

"It was Jill," Mason finally said.

Stace gasped.

Warren looked back to Mason, shocked—fake shocked. "Jill." Warren got up. He walked around frantically and stopped in front of Mason. He suddenly looked like he got it all. He started nodding. His eyes turned to slits. He let out a heavy breath. "You're seriously fucking with me." He shook his head and stared hard at Mason. "Is that what's going on here, Mason?"

Mason stood his ground without a response.

"The problem with that, Mason. I'm not the *fuck with me* type."

Again, Mason had no response for Warren. He was done explaining or trying to get Warren's buy-in, and he wasn't going to stick around for anymore showdowns. That, seriously, wasn't going to get him anywhere. At this point, the only thing Mason could do was keep moving.

He suddenly headed for the door. "Stay close but when my head goes off, disappear. And if you want something in particular to look for, make it a remote." He turned back to Warren just as he was about to leave. He pointed to the walls; the C4.

CHAPTER 43

Mason stepped out from the back door, looking at the field he'd escaped into. There was nothing out here that would help him. He looked over to the other building. It was quiet, dark, and disturbingly suspicious. He could see the windows he looked through before, but they were lifeless now. It seemed as though Dr. Harlow not only cleared everything, and everyone, from the small building; but he evacuated the large one also. Unsure if that was the case, he moved toward it.

He touched his head thinking that if anyone was still here, the device would have blown his mind apart by now. But it hadn't, so they must be alone. He didn't know much about the device in his head—nothing really. He didn't know if it was always activated, or if someone controlled it. Maybe it had been Andrew who had all of that figured out. All he knew about the device was, if it did go off, he would need a remote to stop it.

He kept moving toward the main building. Suddenly, the clang of metal rang out followed by a piercing, then muffled, scream. Mason instinctively grabbed his head, but he knew right away that was not the problem. He spun around to an overturned sewer grate, and Stace struggling with Steve beside it. He was holding a syringe against her neck.

"I knew if you made it back here, you wouldn't be alone. I was hoping for Andrew, but at least you're wearin' his favorite shirt," Steve said while searching in all directions.

Mason showed the gun. "This is all I have to remember him by."

"Oh, your prize for winning the battle? Probably not a good idea for you to have it though." Steve pressed the syringe tighter against Stace's neck.

"She's got nothing to do with this friggin' freak show."

"Yet… We've never tried Purify on someone this ripe."

Mason pointed the gun with his finger on the trigger. What to do was his choice, but the decision wasn't easy. He knew if he shot, there was no telling who the bullet would hit. If it missed completely, Stace would be the next Purify victim with who knows what results. As far as Mason could tell, Stace stood a pretty good chance of coming out the loser, so really, he had no choice.

"Here," He said as he turned the gun around and held it out. "It's all yours."

Steve started to laugh. "Mason, really? I know what you're capable of."

Mason dropped the gun. He cleared his hands away then kicked it toward him. "There, a clean handoff. Just let her go. There's a field she can run into then whatever happens from this point is up to you."

"Mason, whatever happens is already up to me."

"Fine. If that's the way you see it, just let her go. Then you guys get me back."

Steve started laughing. "He doesn't want you back. Didn't we already go through this?"

Mason looked down, unsure what to do. "Okay, so you tell me. What's next?" When Mason looked back up, his eyes scanned past Steve without making it obvious he was looking for something, someone.

Steve looked at the gun lying far enough away from him to make the decision difficult. He started to move toward it while keeping Stace tight in his grasp and his eyes on Mason.

"Let her go, man. The gun's right there," Mason said.

Suddenly, Mason heard a crash behind Steve. Steve turned and Stace broke away. She ran for the field leaving Steve an open target.

Steve went for the gun, but a shot fired. He fell with a single slug in his head.

Warren appeared from behind the garbage bin.

Mason breathed a sigh of relief. He approached Steve—now dead. He picked up the gun, put it back under his waistband, then took the syringe and examined its contents. He let out a sigh not knowing if this could be what was in the capsules. He dropped it and crushed it under the stomp of his boot.

Mason continued to search Steve and found a ring of keys and a remote. He looked at the remote and rubbed his head. He took it as if it were a medal of victory. Then, he looked to the main building as Warren and Stace came up beside him.

Warren said, "What are you thinking, Mason?"

Warren surely doubted all of this before, but Mason knew he was fully on board now. *And thank God for that. Nothing worse than battling two at the same time.*

He looked at the two of them then back to the main building. "We came here looking for Linda," Mason said with authority.

CHAPTER 44

Entry into the main building was easy. First, Mason came to a service door. It wasn't wide open like at the back of the smaller building, but it wasn't locked. There was nothing going on in here that would be figured out easily. Everything he saw at first was empty—the hallway, a supply room near the door, the staff room further down. Everything indicated this place had been completely cleared out. In fact, he would have turned around right away if it wasn't for the vocal battlefield that was impossible to miss.

Ahead of him was a maze of open doors and hallways. The commotion he heard didn't come from anywhere obvious, but it was definitely inside the building. These would be the hallways to take him there if he really wanted to go.

Mason rushed ahead of Warren and Stace. He stopped at another hallway and checked it cautiously. He looked back to them. He thought about waiting but made an instant decision to do this on his own, just in case… "Find the main doors, and make sure they're open." He shot a look at Stace. Hopefully she understood. "It's better this way." He ran off without giving her a chance to respond.

***

Warren stood stunned. He didn't expect Mason to abandon them, but he wasn't going to complain about it either. To Warren, this was his show now, with or without the knowledgeable tour guide. He held his position for a second then started cautiously walking toward the chaos. At this point it was the only direction he could go. The only other choice would be back the way they came. Although leaving was probably not a bad idea, he pursued onward in search of everything Mason promised.

He moved down the hallway without incident. It was just the chaos that was troublesome, which would become a huge problem if he kept wandering. He started down another hallway when he turned around. Stace had stopped at a door, so he went back to her.

Warren looked through the screened glass. Behind it was a reception area. It didn't look like anyone was in the room, and Warren could see the main doors they were looking for.

Stace grabbed the handle. It turned. Warren took her place then cautiously opened the door.

***

Mason saw a closed door up ahead. He figured since all the other doors he passed were wide open, this one must be locked. He reached in his pocket for the keys then tried one. No luck; he tried another. After a few more attempts, he entered. It was a room with medical equipment and beds, just like the ones Dr. Harlow used in his basement lab. None of these beds were used though. They were just there, made up with tight bed sheets.

Mason thought about the beds left abandoned in the basement of the small building. He figured there would be no way Dr. Harlow moved everyone over here. The risk of being in such a large, obvious building was too great. He must have taken the whole operation completely off this site, but he didn't know where that would be. He had only been in the smaller building where even the basement was foreign to him. The constant roar of what sounded like a fight club reminded him that something was left behind though. If nothing else, he should be able to get information about where the doctor went from that, or them, or it…

On the other side of the room, another door was open. He began to go there when someone ran by.

***

Warren made a thorough sweep of the reception area to be sure they were alone. He ended up at the main double doors. He looked out to a parking lot they had driven by when they first got here. This was not the way they went to the smaller building though. A more secluded service entrance seemed more appropriate. He started unlocking the inside set of doors when an old man rushed in.

"My God! They've gone mad," the old man shouted.

Warren turned. The old man saw him, so he stopped, surprised—hyper surprised.

"Who—" He started to tremble.

"Oh, sorry. I knocked. No one…" Warren could see Stace in the room, but the old man hadn't.

The old man made a run for the door he just came from.

Warren rushed to him. "Oh no, Gramps." He pulled him back and showed his badge.

The old man suddenly became confused. First shocked, then afraid, and now confused. Warren thought even he seemed to have trouble keeping it all straight.

"I've done nothing wrong. None of us have," he said. He started shaking again. "Oh no, I shouldn't have said that." He looked at Warren for help. "Did I say something wrong?"

Warren shrugged, not sure how to respond.

"No, no, no one's done anything wrong," Stace said as she stepped in and walked him away from Warren.

That just panicked him more. He trembled but put up no resistance.

Stace looked back to Warren and pointed to a sign on the reception desk—Psychiatric Evaluation and Assessment Center.

The old man calmed down a bit, but he was fixated on the door. "Oh God. We all should have listened to Mason."

Stace said, "Mason? You know Mason?"

Warren noticed he was suddenly relieved.

"Of course. We all know Mason." The relief was short lived, followed immediately with depression—emotional chaos. "But he left us…"

***

Mason quickly moved down the hallway in the same direction he saw the person flee. He couldn't have gone far. There was a corner up ahead, so Mason thought he must be just around that. Mason got there—nobody. *Was he hiding? Did he see me?* Mason was still alone which was definitely not a bad thing, but he thought any second that could change.

He stopped after he passed another room with rows of beds left with their covers messed up. Maybe they were there. Another closed door was across the hall. He grabbed the handle expecting it to be locked. It opened. It was a linen closet packed with bed sheets and surgical gowns. Mason looked down the hall but suddenly realized that the person he followed, came from the same direction he did. He wasn't running from the noise, he was running to it.

Suddenly, he bolted back down the hallway, away from the chaos.

***

Warren was swarmed by a group of frantic people rushing into the reception area followed by a woman, obviously the only coconut still attached to the tree.

"Stanley," she yelled. "Where did you—" She stopped when she noticed the old man with Stace. The group stopped too, like she had them tied on a leash.

"Cops!" Stanley shouted as if everyone should now run for cover.

Instead, Warren watched them stay frozen—guilty but innocence was obvious. He noticed the woman's frustration, but she seemed more concerned about what they were all running from.

"We have to get out."

Stanley pointed at the main doors. "Through those doors, Hazel? That's where I'm going." He moved toward them, but Warren stopped him. Stanley started to panic, uncontrollably.

"Shit." Warren backed off. He turned to Hazel. "More of him down the hall, right?"

Hazel rushed to help. "You don't have to go that far." She looked in all directions.

Warren saw the group splitting up. Hazel attempted to get them under control, but failed not knowing who to go after first. Some went for the door; others rushed toward the hallway. All of them were paranoid and panicking.

Warren blocked the main entrance. He saw Stace guarding the other door. That kept everyone inside but added to the commotion. One guy grabbed a coat rack for a weapon.

Another stormed under the reception desk for cover. A few young girls huddled together, afraid of anyone coming near them.

Warren felt the room had the tension of bending glass, then the yelling started. First from a woman curled up in a corner who started screeching out of control. Others quickly followed until the room itself sounded like it was screaming. "How many people?" Warren shouted.

"That depends how you define people," Hazel said. She was now a cowhand herding insanity. "The others wouldn't leave."

Warren saw Stanley grab a wall phone. Stace stopped him.

Hazel looked back to the hallway with a total loss of control. "Please. We have to—"

"What the hell happened here?" Stace asked, but no one answered.

Warren moved toward the hallway. He turned back. "Just tell me where the fuck Linda is."

Warren was stunned by the sudden silence. Even a toothpick snap would have been deafening.

Stanley started shaking like a cornered squirrel.

Even Hazel looked like she was going to lose it. "Please, please, we have to get out," she said.

Warren stood at the hallway door. He looked to Stace. "Take'm, Stace, and call some cops."

Stace directed them out without hesitation.

"State, not local."

She acknowledged him with a head shake.

"Don't go back there unless you're purified," Hazel said. She headed to the main doors with those she had gathered up.

Warren looked at her curiously. He looked to Stace who was also confused. He watched the completely frazzled group moving for the front doors. He stayed at the other door for a moment longer with his eyes doing the thinking. Then, he left.

***

Mason stood between the two buildings looking at a lifeless Steve. It didn't seem possible, but where else could they be? Considering this would be the action of Dr. Harlow, it was the only answer. He stared at the sewer grate.

As far as Mason knew, Dr. Harlow had two in the program—Linda and the other guy. Dr. Harlow would definitely abandon everyone else but not those two. There was no doubt in Mason's mind that Dr. Harlow would be attached to them, just as he was to him. The beds were left behind, so there was nothing huge he needed. He couldn't have left here completely because they only had the blue van, and that was parked on Maple Avenue now.

And the burning question on Mason's mind was, where did Steve suddenly come from?

***

Warren was alone except for more yelling, banging, and then a deafening scream. It all seemed to be coming from behind a door at the end of the hallway. He rushed to it and kicked it wide open.

Inside was freak show pandemonium.

He saw deformed people guarding three nurses. One nurse lay on a bed that was covered in blood. Another was on the floor and the third hung by her arm caught in window bars. A fourth nurse quivered in a chair. A creature stroked her hair and ran fingers through blood streaming from her neck.

Away from this, he turned to a terrified group. It was likely the group Hazel broke up. Those remaining were either too slow or just plain unlucky. Their biggest problem now was the mental capacity required to get out of here alone. So there they were, fresh picking for what Warren looked at—a group of physical and mental deformities.

He knew this group wasn't concerned about anyone. They were in total control of everything. That was, until they noticed Warren.

All of them watched him with their curiosity rapidly escalating. A few approached him, so he took out his gun. That slowed them but not others moving up from the back of the pack. He backed up against the door. All eyes were on Warren but no help. He was alone, the only one of his kind.

He fired a shot into the ceiling.

***

A long, dark passage faced Mason. Dampness shone on the walls and floor. Mason had two directions to choose from, but the one to take was obvious from the faint hum of a motor and a dim light. He started down but realized he would trap himself if he went farther. The only way out was the way he came in, and that could easily be sealed tight if someone saw him go down.

He shook his head and sighed. He didn't have much choice. He was sure about what was at that light. If it all came down to this dark, dreary place, then so be it. It looked like Dr. Harlow was at the end of his rope, and Mason intended to snap it. *What's the difference if it goes down in a sewer?*

While he was stalled here, leaning against the rounded wall, he realized the grate hadn't been moved; so there was a good chance no one knew he was here. He checked the gun tucked under his waistband. It was there. At least he had something.

He pushed himself away from the wall. He began to walk deeper into a place from which he may never return.

***

Warren had the door open a crack while he held off the freak show. This was the only hope for the hopeless. For now the gun worked, but a hunchback heavyweight with clubs for hands seemed impatient. Warren's eyes locked on him as he tried desperately to wave the terrified group out.

He turned to them. Most were too afraid to move. A few started for the open door. Warren continued waving—faster, to encourage momentum. The others cautiously followed, but no one had made it out yet. They all huddled together in front of the door. It was like leaving scared them as much as being here.

Warren boldly pushed open the door and rushed the group of creatures with his gun stretched out firmly in front of him.

Quasimodo surged with his clubs swinging. Warren didn't hesitate and took him down with one shot. After that, everything went berserk.

Warren lunged for the door, got through behind the last of the frightened, and slammed it shut.

***

Mason stepped softly into an area where light pulsated with the humming generator. No one saw him which gave him a chance to check out the surroundings. Even with the light, darkness remained, and shadows were everywhere.

He quickly made out Dr. Harlow working intensely with a monitor. He held a vial of black serum. He worked beside a guy who was on a gurney. Wires lay all over him. Some were attached and others weren't. He looked as dead as the room itself.

It was hard to believe it all came down to this, Mason thought. He knew Dr. Harlow was determined to see his discovery through to the end. But holed up in a sewer? Mason wasn't sure if this was because of his extreme tenacity or his sure insanity. Probably both, but how could he think this would work out? Possibly, Dr. Harlow's work was done. Was it possible he didn't care where he was because all he set out to accomplish was complete? Mason was an example of success. If he did it again with this guy, then maybe that was it. Maybe Dr. Harlow had what he needed—but wait. Judging by the looks of how Dr. Harlow was acting, that couldn't be the case.

Mason watched Dr. Harlow check a readout from a single machine. He was obviously confused. Violently, he ripped the paper, almost knocking over a homemade C4 explosive sitting beside the machine. He threw the vial.

"Damn, the bastards who put me here." He looked at his patient then to something moving in the corner.

Mason had trouble making it out at first, but as he focused, his eyes adjusted. Slowly, he started seeing tangles of bound legs. He made out a straitjacket that controlled its movements. Gagged with a cloth, its bald head turned desperately to Mason.

Mason knew exactly what he looked at now. He took a step into the room then closer for clarification. *Another, just like me.* But now his cover was gone which quickly became more of a concern.

Dr. Harlow jumped up. Mason knew he was now in full view.

"Mason. Just when I thought you'd never—" He rushed

to him. "Like blossoms in spring." He tried to touch him like a mother would her estranged child.

Mason pushed him away.

"Why, Mason?"

Mason said, "Why? How deep will you go before you steal the last corpse?"

Dr. Harlow smiled. "Stop teasing me with conception." He looked at him shyly then fell down to the corner. "Help me, Mason." He comforted the prisoner.

"You haven't got a clue. You can't see anything beyond your cherished Purify can you?"

"We need to leave here, Mason."

"We're leaving alright. Finally, for you, it's over."

Dr. Harlow looked up, deranged. "Over. No, it's not over." He untied the gag. "You're still just a baby."

The prisoner gasped then groaned, desperately fighting to set itself free from the jacket.

"And Linda, my sweet, precious Linda has just been born."

Linda. Of course. Mason showed his gun.

Dr. Harlow lunged in front of her. "No, Mason. You can't kill her. We need her." Dr. Harlow sprung up and crashed into the gurney on his way back to the machine.

Mason watched the guy roll onto the floor, but Dr. Harlow didn't care. Mason turned to see Linda desperately working herself free. He pointed the gun at Dr. Harlow who took a remote device beside the C4 explosive.

"Mason, help me." He rushed back to Linda.

"No one can help you, but this will help us all," Mason said, determined that this would be the end.

Dr. Harlow looked at Mason. He seemed to understand. He backed up against the wall. His eyes pleaded to Mason. "You need me, Mason." He reluctantly held up the remote. He looked at the C4.

Mason stepped closer, toward him.

Dr. Harlow shied his eyes away, blocking his view with his hand. "Remember, you're dead without me... Mason."

"You've taken everything from me; you've killed my best friend. You've even taken away my right to die." Mason paused—those words weighing so heavily on him. He wasn't sure this would solve all that, but he knew it would definitely stop the madman in front of him. "Sealing your casket is the only help you'll ever get from me."

"Andrew!" Dr. Harlow screamed, suddenly frightened.

"And I'll take death over ever needing you."

"Steve!" Dr. Harlow shouted with terror.

Mason steadied the gun with pressure on the trigger. "Look at me, Harlow. Even you can understand this." The gun was inches away. "I'm not dead."

Dr. Harlow jumped up. He was instantly defensive, instantly confronting—an instant enemy. "Out of my way." He pushed past Mason as though there had never been a gun pointed at him.

That shocked Mason enough to put him off pulling the trigger. He realized he just lost his chance and turned quickly, trying to get his target back. Suddenly, Mason was hit. The gun fell.

Mason shook off the hit and rushed Dr. Harlow who was running for the door. He knocked him down. Mason felt the gun firmly pressed against his head. He noticed Bob Robinson holding it.

Mason watched Dr. Harlow breathing heavily. This was far too much brutality for a frail, old man. He staggered to his feet. He pocketed the remote and left for the tunnel with a deadly stare for Mason and a whistle for himself.

Bob went nowhere though. "Why so much trouble, Mason? How can you turn against your savior, your creator, your God?"

Mason said, "My God? A lunatic who gives life without identity is now called God? Is that a life worth living?"

Mason tried to push past Bob when the butt of the gun dropped him again.

"I think it is, but if you don't, fine."

Mason held his head and watched Bob leave. The room spun. Light pulsated. The generator became deafening. His shirt started to crawl. He grabbed his back, screaming.

Limbs began to break through.

***

Warren burst out from the building. He saw Stace and Hazel still trying to calm the group, but at least they were all out. He rushed toward them and forced the whole group farther away from the doors. He yelled to Stace. "Keep them moving. All the way into the parking lot."

He stopped at the end of the walkway and saw two police cruisers pulling in. Warren turned with his gun drawn.

The pack of enraged creatures emerged from the building. They slowed down because of the doors, but they were practically crawling over each other.

Warren opened fire.

More creatures plowed their way through the door. Warren took some out, but he couldn't keep up. He looked over to one of the cops ready to shoot from behind his cruiser's door. He looked terrified. Warren took out two more. Others bee-lined down the walkway as though expecting a feeding frenzy. Warren looked back at the cop who hadn't done a thing. "Jesus Christ, man!" Warren shouted.

He saw another cop start firing. Warren joined in, and one by one they picked them off until the last reject fell.

***

Dr. Harlow heard the last of the shots as he pulled himself out from the hole. Disoriented outside the sewer, he struggled to get his footing. He was winded terribly, but he still tried to move the sewer grate back over the hole. Unable to budge it, he looked around deciding which way to go. He began staggering toward the main building.

***

Bob ran for the sewer opening. He looked back because of an echoing scream. He pressed harder but still had a considerable distance to cover. He stopped, desperately trying to see another way out. He quickly started for the opening again.

***

Daylight broke as Warren checked for movement in the pile of carnage. Warren turned back when another police car entered the area. He saw that everyone in the parking lot was still shaken up, but at least there was some order now. He started walking there.

Warren stopped with the sound of movement. He snapped back around with his gun up, ready to take down another straggler. He hesitated at the sight of an old man stumbling through the broken up doors. He seemed horrified by the lifeless pile. Warren watched him bend down to them. He cautiously touched them as though afraid to catch what they had. He staggered back against the wall.

"You must be the infamous Doctor Harlow." Warren pressed forward with his finger on the trigger, ready to fire. "Hope you didn't name them."

Dr. Harlow looked wearingly at him. He seemed unconcerned, or possibly even unaware, of the gun pointed directly at him. "You people have no idea what I've done," he said, exhausted by emotion.

"Something only a mother could love?"

Dr. Harlow ignored Warren's sarcasm. "A drug that solves all disease, and I have people, living people, to prove it."

"People… You have real people that you held against their will. You've conducted your research without authorization, and you've killed to protect it."

"I've created perfect human beings, but the world can't deal with that. Can't eliminate cancer, heart disease, AIDS. No, no. Society depends on them."

He trembled. Warren saw his legs shake. He was barely able to hold himself up. Warren stepped closer and lowered his gun. "Tell me about those perfect human beings." He held out his hand, but Dr. Harlow pushed it away. Warren looked down at the carnage all around him. "Where are those people, Doctor?" He looked back at him. "Where's my wife?"

Dr. Harlow ignored the question. "It's just too great. Too great for you or anyone else." Dr. Harlow turned away and dug into his pocket. He pulled out the remote device. He held it up as though Warren should have already known what it was for.

"I know where Mason is, Doctor. I can take you to him, but first tell me where the others are."

"Mason doesn't concern me anymore. Handing you over everything I've created does though."

Warren's eyes widened as he focused on the remote. Suddenly, he held his gun back up—aggressively but uncertain. Panic was in his eyes. "No, Doctor, there are people in there," he said, his voice shaking with fear. He looked around aimlessly. "Where are they?"

"If the world won't have my drug, it'll all be destroyed."

Warren was frantic now. "Doctor, please. Linda's still..." Warren lunged at him in desperation, but Dr. Harlow stood still. He grasped on to the remote.

***

Completely evolved again, Mason worked to free Linda when he heard a clunk. He turned to see the C4 explosive, ticking.

He looked back to Linda who continued to work her way out of the straitjacket. She broke free with too many arms and legs for her to handle. She stopped moving to examine the webs.

Mason said, "Get ready to use them." He helped her up.

She tried to rush to the man but fell. She pulled herself the rest of the way.

Mason looked back at the bomb. "If he's not dead now, he's gonna be." He grabbed her making the decision easy.

"We can't just leave him."

Mason already had her heading for the tunnel. "In a second you won't even remember you said that."

Mason turned the corner into the tunnel. Linda stumbled. Mason practically ran her over, but she quickly got herself moving.

"Use your webs," Mason shouted.

Linda was obviously confused. It was dark, and there was no space. Suddenly, they heard an explosion, but it wasn't down here. Linda ran faster then lifted off slightly.

Mason saw morning light shining from the sewer opening ahead then the glow of fire. Bob's silhouette fell to the ground at the opening.

He moved faster behind Linda. A deafening blast shook the tunnel. Mason looked back to the room, and it was a complete fire ball.

He pushed Linda forcing her to use her webs. She glided gracefully. Mason took another look. The generator was now a ball of fire and coming straight at him. He accelerated then became airborne.

Linda touched down with two steps; the opening was up ahead. She flew low, pulled her legs in then sprung herself straight up into the sewer opening.

Fire glowed all around Mason as he pulled the same move and blasted up the opening. He looked down seeing the generator crash into Bob. He blasted straight up with Linda just above him. A huge swell of fire followed him. He plowed through flying debris from the exploded small building like a missile with no target.

He caught up to Linda, soaring high above the burning building. The sewer he just came from was split wide open. The main building was untouched. He looked at her, not quite sure what to make of this. He saw the parking lot; lights flashed from police and emergency vehicles. People moved around frantically. He started to fall gracefully with Linda, toward the back of the untouched building.

He landed. She opened her hand with a look—not sexual but dependent. She dug a fingernail into her palm.

Black blood dripped. She held it up to Mason's mouth, and he instinctively took it with his tongue.

CHAPTER 45

Warren fought to get through police officers gathered around him. They struggled to hold him back from entering the blast zone.

"Detective, come on, man. There's nothing in there for you," a cop said in an attempt to calm him. "Over here." He tried to lead him away. "We'll think this through."

Warren surged again, but he was constrained. He pleaded with the cop holding him back. "It's my wife in there. I have to—" He surged again.

"No, Detective, she's not. No one's back there."

Reluctantly, Warren gave in. He turned away to the parking lot full of patients, police officers, police cars. He looked back to the main building. Grief overwhelmed him. He grabbed his head and crashed down on his knees.

He felt Stace beside him. She bent down and held him by

the shoulder. He looked up with his face messed from tears and dirt. She was the same. She stayed there. He was comforted by her and consumed by his grief. All the emergency activity around him did nothing to break his sorrow. His loss was personal, and his pain permanent.

Warren heard someone yell from the parking lot.

"Over there. In the building."

Warren looked. Working their way through debris from the doors and fallen creatures, Mason and Linda, dressed in surgical gowns, looked out. Both were alive.

Warren closed his eyes then opened them again. He smiled, jumped up, and ran to Linda.

He saw her crying as she worked her way through the doors. He held her, instantly a new man. He touched her face then her bald head. Tears ran down his face.

***

Mason saw Stace watching. He walked slowly to her.

"You need to find a new place to buy clothes," Stace said.

Mason looked at what he wore, smiled, then he hugged her. His eyes met hers, and he gave her a kiss. He shared another moment then passionately embraced her.

***

Warren noticed a cruiser holding Dr. Harlow begin to shake. Shaking turned to pounding then the windows blew out. A back door flew from the car and Dr. Harlow emerged.

He was far away. Others closer fled from his path. Officers froze in shock. Warren was stunned from what he was looking at. He looked curiously at Linda's head.

Dr. Harlow made a straight surge directly for Mason who was still lost in the moment with Stace.

Warren went for his gun; there were too many people. He moved for a clear shot.

Dr. Harlow approached quickly without obstruction. Warren panicked while trying to clear people out of the way. It was too late.

Warren yelled, "Mason!"

***

Mason looked up; he turned. A gun flew toward him. He caught it and looked the other way. Dr. Harlow was almost on top of him.

He shot; a direct hit.

Dr. Harlow fell at his feet. Mason dropped the gun as Warren and Linda approached. He grabbed his hand that held the gun. He looked at it.

Mason noticed Warren overwhelmed with confusion by the sight of Dr. Harlow. His limbs, the webs, his hairlessness...

Stace touched Mason's arm then led him away. Mason saw her turn to look at Dr. Harlow. He saw her eyes meet Warren's. Both of them were speechless.

Mason wiped his hand on his gown, leaving a black smear. He looked back at Linda who watched him. He knew they were two on the edge of evolution.

###

ABOUT THE AUTHOR

I often wonder why I remember meeting some people but not others; recall some events but not all. I remember the exact time I met my brother-in-law, but I don't know when I first saw my wife. I recall clearly the start line of my first marathon, but I can't seem to remember the end of the one I just finished.

I guess it all has to do with knowing, at the time, how significant that person or event will be. I didn't know my wife would be my wife, but I did know that first marathon wouldn't be my last.

In October, 2004, while driving along a busy highway, I came up with my first story concept. It wasn't this story, but it was my first. The event is clear in my mind; the story is still fresh. I know why I remember it so vividly. I knew right then, this event would change my life.

From there my adventure into story telling had begun, and

it couldn't have happened at a better time. I had been thrust into adulthood with the responsibility of marriage and three kids. I knew what I had to do, and embracing corporate culture was the plan. But that fell apart when the company I worked for started to fail. Corporate downsizing, pay cuts, severance packages, and buyouts were subjects of conversations that filled the air. When the axe swung, we all ducked then looked up to see who got cut.

I started writing—a proactive new plan that involved creativity. It wasn't long before I realized the power of that word—creativity. It had been in me all along, but life simply got in the way. Creativity was only one part of the writing equation though. It's true what they all say—writing isn't easy.

I started that first story as a screenplay. There were less words in a formatted, one hundred page script; and who could turn away from the inevitable blockbuster that would result. The naive writer had begun, and a disastrous story was the result. But I'm not a quitter. An education in story and writing was daunting, but I dove in with my eyes wide open.

Twelve finished screenplays resulted and many other stories were conceived, outlined, started... Purified was one of the finished screenplays. It started out as a story called Wonder Drug. Rewrites changed the name to Purify. Finally, the title became Purified. Each one of those titles were compressed, expanded, elevated, and finalized. When I stepped away from screenwriting, Purified was the story I decided to pursue as my debut novel.

That pursuit was supported with a strong understanding of story and required more education in writing. Point of view, verb tense, sentence structure, and many other skills were required for the changeover to writing novels. Oh yes, also word count...

I persevered, and now Purified is published.

Like crossing the finish line of a marathon, writing this means my debut novel is done. Like standing on the start line of that first long distance race, I'll remember this moment because I know it won't be my last.